SHADOWLANDS SECTOR

TWO

MILA YOUNG

DEDICATION

To my friends who always listen to me babbling about story ideas when I need a sounding board, to my editors for being incredibly talented and bring out the shine in my stories, and to my Beta readers who give invaluable insight and I love chatting with always.

Love you
Mila

CONTENTS

Shadowlands Sector One
Shadowlands Sector Two
Shadowlands Sector Three

SHADOWLANDS SECTOR TWO

It's only a matter of time before I destroy them all...

A raging, bloodthirsty wolf isn't the only deadly thing inside me. So, I have to do what I've always done best. Run.

Leaving my alphas and the first taste of love I've ever known is the only answer now.

And even when Fate steps in and puts us all back together, including a sexy new alpha with troubles of his own, I can't stay. Even though it's killing me to go.

The pain of being away from them will literally kill me, but no matter what happens to me, I can't let them pay for my weakness.

I can't save myself, but I can save them. I can save them from seeing what I will become...

But my dominant alphas are better hunters than I am prey, and they're determined to keep me...whatever the cost.

CHAPTER 1

MEIRA

"Don't cry. Don't you dare cry!" I mutter under my breath, yet a sob sticks to my throat as my insides rip to shreds with heartbreak.

I'm running for my life through the forest, leaping over dead logs, ducking under low branches, never stopping. The sounds of screams and growls fill the woods behind me, and I can't stop shaking.

All I can think about are my Alphas. The two men I gave myself to, who protected me, who marked me. And now I'm fleeing from them. But I have no choice…because they know the truth.

I try to erase the images of the bloodshed between the Ash Wolves and Shadow Monsters, but they stain my mind. I remind myself I'm immune to the infected who plague this world, and remaining with the Ash Wolves will only bring war to their doorstep. Every wolf shifter will fight to claim a part of me for themselves, believing I can somehow make them resistant to the virus. I don't even know if that's true, but it won't stop the wolves from trying. Desperation drives everyone to madness.

I flashback to a memory of Lucien saying, *"If such an elixir existed, it would end in bloodshed."* He's right… and I won't be responsible for starting a war amongst the wolves. It doesn't help that I'm a half-human, half-wolf and still haven't had my first fucking transformation into a wolf. Not even after two Alphas marked and mated with me.

That makes me a liability. If my wolf decides to show, it will rip out of me, killing me, and then it will slaughter everyone in sight. For those two reasons, I run to spare everyone the atrocities I'll bring to their home. Me escaping is offering them an opportunity to forget me, no matter how much fear closes my throat at the thought of never seeing my Alphas again.

My eyes water, and my insides shiver.

I'm doing the right thing.

I feel like shit on the inside for running, but I also know an opportunity to save lives when I see it. I don't belong in this pack. As much as my heart splinters in protest, I need to be clever and think about the consequences my actions will have. The knot in my chest tightens, and I swipe at the falling tears, my breaths turning to choked cries.

There's an ocean of undead pouring into Dušan's fortress. There's been a breach in the wall, and now the monsters infiltrate his compound. My gut clenches at the thought of innocents dying, but the Ash wolves are the toughest sons of bitches I've ever met. If anyone can survive such an onslaught, it's them.

Savage growls punch through the normally silent woods.

My chest feels ripped open and bleeds with agony for stealing away from them. A sudden flare of pain simmers through my body, deepening with each breath. Except I can't be sick again, not here and not now, so I fight past the screaming hurt.

I suck in each ragged breath and keep running, even though I feel like shattered glass.

Lanky, infected creatures bump into me in a frenzy to reach the wolf pack. I shoulder past them, shoving them aside, then I pick up a thick branch and cringe at the sting shooting up my side. But I don't waste the moment. I use it to take down a few creatures, slamming the weapon into their faces, sending them onto their backs. I thrust the branch into mushy, soft brains, the slushy sound sickening. I destroy half a dozen before the cluster heading to the pack fades behind me. I drop my branch covered in goo and blood, then dart away.

Screams and war cries bleed into the day, but I don't look back anymore. The Ash Wolves are my past, and I can only look forward. It's the only way I'll survive, even if my heart breaks. This isn't the time for emotions. I need to be strong and rational with every action I take.

My lungs ache and scream for oxygen when I reach the deep woods. I rest near an oversized oak tree, laying my hands on my knees and leaning over as I suck in deep pockets of air. My inhales wheeze, sweat coats me, and every muscle trembles. I squeeze my eyes shut tightly, the tears refusing to stay at bay, and I hug myself as I stumble into the tree at my back.

My time with the Alphas plays on my mind, and the memories just won't go away. I open my eyes to the trees and bushes surrounding me, the sounds of war replaced by utter silence and the occasional squawk of a bird. No scent of the wolves or infected. Still, the guilt of not helping them more sits on me like a mountain.

"Helping others is a weakness," one of the women I used to share a cave with once said. *"Danger comes, you run. Look after yourself because no one else will."*

I wrap my arms around my middle, remembering the enduring look in Lucien's eyes when he talked to me about his past, when he held me so close I couldn't breathe from desire. Dušan made me feel things no one else ever has, and he promised to keep me safe.

I had let myself believe them, but that was me fooling myself and them. Mama used to say promises are just disappointments waiting to happen.

I draw in deep breaths and stay there long enough to fill my lungs. I'm exhausted by these thoughts, and I can't keep dwelling on them, so I square my shoulders and make myself a promise to forget everything. Just as I have with everything else in my life.

Except my throat closes up and tears burn my eyes. I blink them away and stare at a rock face ahead of me, beaming under the glow of the sun. I see everything, every thin crack… every scurrying ant. I rub my arms, remembering how close I came to shifting… how I still feel my wolf stirring inside me. But getting her to make an appearance, even with the Alphas' help, just refuses to happen.

I don't need anyone. I keep repeating that in my mind like a mantra, hoping it will sink in. I push away from the tree and leap into a jog, putting more distance between me and them… *Swift and silent.*

The rest of the day, I keep moving, not knowing where I'll end up. But that doesn't matter, as long as it's as far from the wolves as possible. I've lived this long without them, and I'll continue to do so.

My heart gives a heavy thump at the thought.

By the time the sky darkens with the approaching night, I'm staggering, barely able to stay upright, and I stop near a river. I don't recognize the location or even how close I am to where I was living before. That place I'd marked out, where I knew I'd be safe from rogue wolves. But out here, I'm an open target.

I drop to my knees in front of the river and splash my face, then take my fill.

A branch snaps on the opposite bank, and I jerk

my head up, frozen in place. But it's only an infected staggering about. A young girl, maybe thirteen, wearing tattered clothes and only one shoe. Her braids are messy and stained with dark patches. Eyes void of life, she lingers on the spot as if trying to sense where to find her next meal. An animal, a human, a wolf shifter. It's all the same to her. But only the cry of a bird sounds in these woods.

She looks right through me like I am one of her kind, undetectable and non-existent. I climb to my feet and dust the dirt from the knees of my black leggings, while water stains splash my wrap-around blue top.

I scan the trees for the best sleeping location. Up there, I'm safe from rogue wolves and other creatures that come out at night to scour the woods. I have no weapons to defend myself, so I move quickly, having no time to waste. I scramble forward and use a tree's rough edges and lower branches to scale the trunk until I reach a natural platform made of three branches. At least twenty feet off the ground, I sit with my back to the trunk and fold my legs in front of me. Not the best spot, but it'll do. I survived for five years on my own, and I can do it again.

Deep breath, I remind myself and think back to the last time I scaled a tree for protection… It was the first time Dušan found me in the woods, when I should have run and never let him into my life. My bones seem to tremble at the memory of him close to me, his presence and scent swallowing me, claiming me before he ever marked me.

I reach up to the back of my neck where he bit me. The skin is smooth now, but the flesh feels sensitive under my fingertips.

After everything I've gone through—watching my mama be eaten by the infected, battling rogue wolves, and being captured—I was mistaken to think I might have found my fated mates.

Because there are no such things for me.

CHAPTER 2

DUŠAN

You fucking sonofabitch... I unleash a growl, the sound thundering across the terrain, doing nothing to stop the onslaught of the infected. Dead, filthy things who are incapable of thinking but are always starved for flesh and blood race through the broken wall into my pack's yard.

I lunge at two of the bastards in my wolf form, my thoughts a mangled blur. On all fours, I charge headfirst and slam into one of their chests, tossing it aside, then snap around, teeth bared at the other culprit. I bite into his leg and tear it off, the slurping sounds nothing but a war song surrounding us.

Everyone will fight until we have slain every

last fucking undead. Armed guards stand on the balcony of our fortress and take down one undead after another. *Bang. Bang. Bang.* They thin the herd as much as possible.

I leap from one creature to the next, taking down as many as I can, tearing the infected from wolves who have fallen. The screams are the worst, but Lucien has my back and we're fighting like a well-oiled machine. We've been at war against these monsters before, battling side by side since we were children.

The world is fucked. But we've adapted, become the killers we need to be. I feel nothing but hatred; everything else grows numb.

Bardhyl barrels into the fight, pelt white as snow charging in from the side of the house. He's a tank, taking down half a dozen creatures in one move. He's the most terrifying bastard I know. It's why I keep him close to my side.

Lucien releases a tremendous growl, and nothing will stop him once he's battling. Bodies scatter the ground around us, limbs twitching, eyes on decapitated heads blinking. But not much scares me anymore.

Wolves fight side by side, and I rip apart the creatures, leaving a pile in my wake. A scream rings through the air, and I swing my head in its direction to my right, my lips peeled back over fangs. Two infected have a female wolf pinned to the ground, biting into her body, ripping away flesh.

Fury slices me in half, and I'm flying toward them. I pounce on one and sink my teeth right into its back, ripping away flesh and bones. In my head, all I can picture is Meira being attacked. She's out there somewhere, and I need to get to her before it's too late.

Stupid woman… she never should have run.

She had so many secrets up her sleeve, didn't she?

One, she has leukemia, and her human body is dying. But I doubt she knows that.

Two, Meira is immune to the zombies because of the disease in her blood. I don't think her blood can be used as a cure, yet she runs because she thinks everyone will hunt her down for it.

Fuck! When I catch her, I'm spanking that tight ass so hard.

I throw myself at the second infected, my teeth latching around its neck, and I take its head right off with sheer rage.

I stare down at the female wolf I recognize as a

new Beta who only recently found her mate. She's on the ground, gurgling blood while it pours out from the edges of her mouth. Her eyes peer into the sky, already turning glassy. There's nothing I can do for her. Once she dies, she'll reawaken as one of them. It's how the virus exists, how it expanded to infect the whole planet. Earth is nothing but a fraction of what it once was.

Nothing remains now. Only the virus-ridden creatures and survivors like us, trying to make a home amid the destruction.

When the Beta quiets down, I snap my jaw around her neck and rip her apart. I don't think about it. Just do what must be done. My brain sits barren for those few moments, choosing to ignore that these images will haunt my dreams for years to come.

But as the Alpha, I won't allow more of the creatures to be spawned. And sure as fuck not from wolves in my family pack.

Then I lunge into battle, forgetting every single fucking thing except destroying the enemy.

We fight.

Undead and wolves fall alike.

I don't pay attention as I plow through the dwindling masses.

I spin around on all fours, searching for my next victim, the heavy scent of blood blotting my senses.

All I find are wolves standing, injured and bloody, while the ground is littered with the undead.

I suck in jagged breaths, refusing to register to the small details. When I glance over to the broken wall and no more undead stagger inside, I tilt my head to the sky and call my wolf back with an ear-shattering howl that bleeds into the air. My flesh ripples as electricity pops over me like sparks. Black fur shrinks, bones crack, and I shudder with the transformation that rips through me in a split second. An explosion of pain swallows me, the agony excruciating, but I'm used to it now. Our changes are vicious.

Getting up to my feet, I stand in the form of a man wearing no clothes and stare out over the chaos. My third and fourth, Lucien and Bardhyl, take human form too, as do others. Bardhyl's white-blond hair flutters in the wind over his broad shoulders, and the way he studies the battle-field reminds me of the first time I encountered him up in Denmark, after he'd single-handedly slaughtered a small pack of Alphas. Lucien should have been my brother, as we are more similar than either of us would admit. He helps someone to their feet, then looks up to me. His steel-gray wolf eyes glint in the sun, and he runs a hand through his short, timber-colored hair.

Then the cries around us begin as wolves begin searching for their loved ones. My gut aches at the grieving sounds.

Lucien steps over a body to reach me. "God-damn fucking infected." His expression twists with hatred as he takes in the massacre.

"We won. That's what counts," I say. "Arrange for all able wolves to take stock of how many we lost, and make sure they are really dead before families take them for burial. Take the rest of the infected down the mountain and as far from here as possible before their rotting bodies reek the air."

He nods, his attention sweeping over the fallen, his face splattered with blood.

"Bardhyl," I call out to the Viking wolf. "We need the wall mended immediately. See to it."

He taps his chest twice with his fist and turns abruptly to the wall. I have faith in my men to get things done. I swing to the dead, and Lucien and I start searching for wolves. They will be reunited with their families before receiving a proper farewell.

I spot a familiar face several feet away. It's a younger Alpha whose brain has been smashed in, meaning this brave soldier won't morph into a creature.

Bang.

The sound from behind me makes me flinch, and I lift my head, hating how fucking jumpy I feel. The guards are making sure all dead wolves stay that way.

We begin collecting the bodies and clearing out the mess. I don't keep track of how long we've been at this, but night starts to stain the sky and my muscles strain.

"We rest now." Lucien is behind me, his body covered in dirt and blood. Getting infected blood into our system doesn't turn us until we die. In truth, we're probably all infected already; many believe it spread through the air so long ago. And now it just lingers inside us until we perish and reawaken.

Around us, only the blood-soaked ground remains. The infected have been piled into trucks for disposing of tomorrow, and wolves are laid in the great hall for family ceremonies.

My head spins with so much to do, except this isn't even close to being over.

Meira comes to mind, and I look up to where the wall at the side of my yard lays smashed open. I keep picturing her running away, pushing past the infected, her gaze meeting mine with utter shock.

The look in her eyes screamed regret, guilt, and heartbreak—but still, she left. Except she never understood the pack rules of mating and marking. Now that she's been marked, she will feel the apprehension and a deep pain in her chest the farther she is from her mates. The problem is that because her wolf hasn't come out, hasn't accepted me or Lucien as her true Alphas, she's susceptible to other wolf attacks. Her slick heat will drive other Alphas to madness to claim her… and she's run out there alone.

"We need to find her." Lucien voices my thoughts. "The leukemia will claim her human body in a week or two."

A deep growl rumbles in my chest. I fucking hate this constant battle. If it isn't one thing, it's another. "We'll go after her tonight," I bark.

He doesn't protest because, like me, he feels the lacerating ache tightening around his chest from being away from his marked mate. I can barely acknowledge that he mated with my Omega, except it's not unheard of for females to pick more than one mate. But I shove those thoughts out of my head for now.

"Help Bardhyl and get ready. We leave in an hour and pray to the moon we're not too late."

"There's something you need to know," Lucien starts, but I shake my head, not ready to hear anything else right now. I'm tired of smelling like blood from the dead and need to get my head straight to work out how the fuck this happened before I take on any more shit.

Meira

A scream bleeds through the night, ripping me from my sleep. My breaths stutter in my lungs.

I rock sideways, my eyes flipping open, and my heart lurches to the back of my throat as I start falling out of the tree. Frantically, my gaze sweeps over the edge of the branch, and I lash out to snatch onto the limb overhead and steady myself. It takes a few moments for my heart to calm down and to make sense of where I am and why. Memories steamroll over me, crashing with incredible speed as I remember the insanity of what I've been through. But what I hate most of all is how easily my heart clenches at the thought of Dušan and Lucien. I'm not stupid—I know their marking me has done something to me, bound us somehow—but I don't understand the rules of how this works. Will the burrowing ache in my chest eventually fade, or will it drive me so mad I'll run back to them? So much for pretending I'll be fine alone. Even here they affect me.

Another scream rings out in the air, this time clearly coming from near the river. It's female, that much I can tell. I stiffen, a sliver of my survival instinct returning.

Is the girl facing a rogue Alpha or a small group of them? What if it's a trick by Mad to find me? Or is it a decoy sound Dušan is using to lure me out of my hiding spot? I can't stop thinking about the last words Mad said to me before I fled.

"I know what's in your blood, why the infected don't touch you."

His words stay with me. They cling to my mind

like thorns, reminding me that to wolves, I'll always be one thing: a lab experiment.

All fantastic reasons for me not to move from my tree. This is how I survived so many years—by butting out of everyone's business. Maybe that makes me gutless, but I prefer to think it's smart.

Another scream, and this time, I chew on my lower lip, my mind starting to think things it shouldn't. Like contemplating ways to sneak down undetected to just see what's going on. But I wait a bit longer…

When the next ear-splitting scream comes, I start moving, climbing down the tree.

I remind myself helping a bit *will* reduce the guilt chewing on my insides at doing nothing.

I have no idea when I changed… the old me would never have done this.

My feet gently kiss the grassy ground, and when no one charges toward me, I slip forward and cut through the night. This better not be a mistake.

Pulling into a dark location under a massive pine, I stare out to the river, where shadows move about.

Someone's backing away, holding what looks like a sword. I squint. Nope, it's a branch.

I hold tight, sinking against the tree. My heart trips over itself, but I'm as silent as the night.

In a split second, the figure spins and runs in my direction, several others chasing right after her. I shudder, my brain firing off sparks and commands to run, but I don't dare move.

The girl darts past me, crying out, while three Shadow Monsters charge after her. Well, her first mistake was making a sound. It only attracts more of those things.

I breathe deeply and crouch, patting the ground. Finding a long branch, I snap it over my knee to create a sharpened point on one end. Then I lunge after the girl. The only reason I'm helping is because I feel shitty enough as it is, running from the pack, and everyone needs a helping hand sometimes.

Running after them, I come up on a shorter undead first and jab the pointy end of the branch into the back of its neck with ferocity. The sharpness cuts deep, breaking skin and sliding into him. Thing about the infected is, their bones and bodies are a lot softer than living creatures', so they're easier to penetrate.

It shrieks and falls over. Plucking the stick out with a gooey sound, I leap over him and run after the second one, shoving the weapon right into its back. A kick to the back of the knees, and the undead lurches forward, falling onto hands and knees. I shove my foot against its spine and grip the branch sticking out of its back. Then I drive down through its supple body and into the soft ground, pinning it in place. I have no idea if it will stay, but I swing and sprint after the girl's screams while stealing another branch off the ground. It's thinner than the last weapon, and the wood feels harder to the touch.

Trepidation crawls up my spine. This is madness on my part, running at night where other predators, including rogue wolves, lurk. But she's making enough noise to wake up the entire mountain.

So I scramble forward, where it's so dark I can barely make out my own hands. My foot catches on a root and suddenly I'm tripping forward, my pulse racing with fright.

I slam into someone, crashing into them hard.

Panic squeezes my lungs and a scream rises out of my throat.

But when the guttural growl of an infected spills into the night from the person beneath me, I quickly scramble back and plunge my weapon into the back of its head, where it's softest, over and over as the creature bucks and fights to get out from under me. But I don't pause, not even when something wet coats my hands.

When it quiets down, I finally stop and just sit there, straddling a dead infected, gasping for air.

I hate this day so much!

I don't know what took over me, as I've never reacted this way before—never acted so aggressively.

A sniffle comes from up ahead, and I lift my gaze to a dark bundle crouching near an oversized shrub.

"Are you okay?" I ask as I push myself to my feet and wipe my hands down my pants. "I'm not going to hurt you, I promise."

Slowly, I creep forward when a young girl steps out. She's maybe thirteen or fourteen years old... God, she's just a child. She only reaches my shoulders in height.

When foliage snaps behind me, I snatch her hand, drawing her to my side. "Shh. No words. Swift and silent, okay?"

She nods, and we both dart to the closest tree with low branches I can find. I swallow hard and help lift her, pushing her butt to climb up faster. I was her age when I lost my mama and had to survive alone in this world. With that thought, a terrible sorrow slivers over my heart at everything I've lost.

More than anything, I long for my Alphas right now, so agonizingly hard that I feel like my chest is cracking in half.

CHAPTER 3

LUCIEN

Dušan charges across the blood-stained field and vanishes in the fortress compound. Everything is fucked, and somehow amid all the chaos, Meira has run from us. I grit my teeth, and my wolf shoves against my insides at the thought that we're letting her get away. She's defenseless, sick, and so damn stubborn that it will get her killed if we don't find her in time. So we need to do everything here fast, because I need her in my arms again.

My stomach tightens each time I think of her against me, her hypnotic scent, the mark that binds us. But it means shit if she goes and gets herself killed. She only had to give us a chance to explain what's in her blood, but she ran. I want to kiss all that fear she carries out of her system.

Stupid woman has no idea how sick she really is or how close to the razor-sharp edge of death she walks.

As far as I'm concerned, we mend the wall and put the pack at ease, find that turd Mad, then go hunting for Meira. I growl, as the to-do list seems impossible.

And it's no coincidence Dušan's second-in-command appears just as everything falls into chaos. He visited the X-Clan pack across the other side of Europe, as Dušan has a trade agreement with them. But we were recently informed by their Alpha, Ander, that Mad stole serum from their compound.

The members of the X-Clan are a different breed of wolves compared to Ash Wolves, and something in their bodies allows them to be immune to infected blood. They have a serum that works only on their kind.

So that fuckhead Mad believed it was an immunity serum and that he could replicate it to use for himself. Except the serum is useless on Ash Wolves, and now his actions are jeopardizing our relationship with our strongest trader.

Dušan knows I want to rip Mad's head off, but he keeps protecting the bastard because Mad is his stepbrother. As far as I'm concerned, Mad deserves shit. They are related only by their parents mating after their were born. There is no biological link whatsoever

Anyway, that doesn't mean Mad's not a dangerous fuck. He is responsible for the shit that went down today. I don't know how, but I'd stake my life on it. He's got shifty eyes. Bardhyl laughs at me when I say this, but you can tell a wolf's true intention by their eyes. They are the mirror into the soul, after all.

So how the fuck did Mad breach the wall to our compound? I don't know the answer, so I storm across the open grounds. Up ahead, the stone barricade lays tumbled inward as though something charged into it from outside. A large chunk remains intact, which should make putting it back together easier.

I push past the pack members collecting loose stones and rubble, and I step into the woods surrounding our home. Blood hangs ripe in the air from the battle, so picking up other scents here is close to impossible. But the tire tracks tearing up the terrain leading up to the wall are a dead give-away. This is the only location with a clearing of woods, so it'd be easy to bring a vehicle up here and smash down the wall, then rapidly drive away before anyone really notices.

"Lucien," Bardhyl bellows. "Get your ass over here and give us a helping hand."

I turn to find him and half a dozen pack members standing in front of the fallen wall, most crouching low to start lifting it back into place.

"Of course."

My hands press to the stone barricade, and we push the goddamn slab upward.

I grunt and strain with the weight, but it doesn't take long for the wall to sit where it once was. Enormous gaps and cracks litter the broken wall, but it's nothing a lot of patching won't help.

Everyone's running around, cleaning up the mess, arranging for families to see to their deceased. Bardhyl turns to me, dust in his long, blond hair and across his brow. He stands slightly taller than me and could have easily stepped out of Viking times. This wolf is a warrior at heart and looks like one. He also has every available female chasing him in the pack... even taken women pay him too much attention. He fucking loves it, and who wouldn't? He's Dušan's fourth and my closest friend, next to Dušan.

I lift my chin for him to follow me out of earshot of others, and we move to the middle of the field where no one stands.

"Have you seen Mad anywhere?" Bardhyl's question comes in the form a growl as his gaze sweeps the yard around us.

I shake my head. "Dušan doesn't even know he's back yet. I didn't get a chance to tell him. But that dickhead won't be far, and he'll be lucky if I don't snap his neck when I catch him."

"I say we find him and chain him up before he gets a chance to do any more damage," Bardhyl growls, the muscled cords in his neck pulsing. His eyes sweep over to me. "Also, Dušan told me you and he are going to hunt down Meira. I want in. We capture Mad, then we head out. I know these woods inside out, and I have her scent. We split in three and cover more ground."

He's my equal, and I have no objection to more of us searching for Meira before it's too late, because it's killing me to know she's out there and we still haven't left our home. But I'm not sure Bardhyl is thinking this through. With Mad returned, someone needs to remain here to lead the pack.

"I know that look," he snaps at me. "Mad didn't fight alongside us, and that makes him the enemy in my eyes. We search for him now and start inside the fortress. We never should have trusted him."

"We didn't, but Dušan..." My words trail off because nothing is ever black and white. They are stepbrothers. Mad and Dušan are the only family each other has, even if not by blood, and those kinds of relationships are the most complicated. I breathe heavily, with dark thoughts sliding over my mind from when my first mate, Cataline, died... I still wake up in a sweat, swearing I can sense her near me. I vowed to never love again, but fate is unpredictable because she's made Meira my fated mate as well. And dealing with those emotions tears me up.

"If we do this, we move fast and grab that bastard," Bardhyl instructs, snapping me out of my thoughts.

I curl my hands into fists, and my heart surges into a race with the promise of a hunt. "Meira is running out of time, and we can deal with Dušan's wrath later if he doesn't like how we deal with Mad."

My friend nods, and we both lunge toward the fortress.

Dušan

We lost seven warriors during the battle, our home has been compromised, and the pack will go into a panic now. They don't feel safe, so it's my job to reassure them and ensure their fortress remains secure.

Though deep in my gut, worry clenches at me. Someone sabotaged us, and I'm going to rip their head off when I find them. Coupled with Meira running away, this whole catastrophe couldn't have come at a worse time.

I emerge from the shower and wipe down the water from my body with a towel, then I drag on my jeans and step into boots. I reach for a clean black tee and tug it over my head and down my body.

If I'm going to address my pack and help them calm down, I'm not doing it covered in blood. They need to know that despite today's tragedy, things will get easier. They have to. I need to believe this, because I can't charge into the woods after Meira if I'm worried about my pack's safety. The longer I take, the farther she'll travel, so I need to move fast.

I march out of my room and down the corridor. My plan had been to work with Meira and find a way to bring out her wolf before her time ran out. If she could just shift, her wolf would heal the blood disease that's ravaging her human side.

Well, that plan had failed miserably. Just thinking about it has me balling my hands into fists, my muscles throbbing with frustration.

Why run, little one?

From the corner of my eye, I notice a figure on the balcony as I pass the doorway. I turn to take a second look. Short cropped white hair. He's in all black, his hands gripping the railing as he stares out to the yard below, where everyone else is working tirelessly to bring back some semblance of normality.

My bristles rise, and my wolf shoves forward with aggression, growling in my chest. My blood boils as I charge toward him.

"You no longer pay your Alpha respect after a mission?" I roar.

Mad whips around to face me, his movement fast, but his smile slow.

My nostrils flare, and I march right up to him, face to face, and I'm breathing down on him. I'm trembling to rip him apart for defying me.

Hostility pours off him, fueling my anger, charging the air with electricity. His eyes narrow with a primal challenge. His mouth pulls into a sneer, accentuating the healed scar on his jawline.

"You stole from Ander." I spit the words in his face. "What the fuck were you thinking? Hand over the serum!" I roar. He's lucky I haven't ripped off his head yet.

My whole trade agreement depends on me returning the serum to the X-Clan. I don't plan to lose the ability to gain new technology and resources from Ander just so Mad can try to play god. This little shit has always looked out for himself. For so long, I justified his actions by telling myself he's younger than me, so he's still got a lot to learn. But this latest stunt might end my patience for him. I've had enough of saving his ass every time he does shit like this.

Mad doesn't move, instead looking me in the eyes, challenging me. "I did this for us," he snaps, like *I'm* the unruly one. "I saw an opportunity and I took it."

I grasp his neck, squeezing. "This isn't a fucking joke."

When I glare into his pale blue eyes, all I can see is my father. In my head, I hear him yelling at me, slapping me in the back of the head and telling me that I'm not good enough. That I'll never make a good Alpha because I'm too weak. Mad would crouch in the corner, whimpering while I got beaten, trying a few times to stop our father. But now he's changed, no longer the stepbrother I grew up with, but a wolf looking for his own path. And I wish him every fucking luck, but it's not going to happen under my roof.

He shoves a hand against my chest, and I release him as he stumbles to find his footing. His lower back presses into the metal railing, cracking a wry smile. "It wasn't like I could call you while in enemy territory and discuss stealing an antidote that could help all Ash Wolves."

That smirk and his words are like gas on my fury. "X-Clan is not the fucking enemy. If you're incapable of understanding a treaty, then I've wasted my time making you my second."

"Dušan," he growls. "That's not fair, man. I did this for us."

My heart slams in my chest, my adrenaline a ticking time bomb about to go off under my ribcage. "You did this for yourself. Otherwise, you would have told me. Instead, I heard it from Ander." A snarl spews past my lips, and he flinches at first, then straightens his shoulders, as if finding his bravery.

He's shaking his head.

I snatch his jaw and squeeze until he winces. "Listen very carefully so your brain understands: The serum from X-Clan does not work on Ash Wolves. It's made specifically for their wolves. It has no effect on us. If you'd asked me, I would have told you that before you went and almost ruined our relationship with Ander."

His eyes grow as wide as the moon at my revelation, and this is why I'm ready to tear off his head. I put him as my second for one simple reason: he's my stepbrother, and I believed he could step up and take the role seriously, keep the Ash Wolves leadership in the family. But that was a mistake, and I won't be making it again.

He yanks back from my grasp, bumping into the railing, a snarl peeling his lips back. "Fuck, fine, you can have them back. Get the hell out of my face."

I shake my head, my fingers curling with the urgency to beat sense into him, though I doubt it would make much difference. I see clearly now the mistake I made by giving my stepbrother this kind of power in the pack.

"Tell me what happened with the delivery of women to Ander. How did you lose one?" I stand tall, my voice rising and patience thinning.

He shrugs. "No idea, but I'd say it's fate considering that little bitch has blood that could be our cure." He leans closer. "Think of the possibilities, brother. I'll take one for the team and fuck her to claim that Omega's cunt, and we use her blood for the cure to help all Ash Wolves."

I'm fuming and throw my fist into his face without hesitation. I clip him in the head, and he lurches backward from the strike, clutching the side of his face. His wolf awakens behind his gaze.

That's what I want... for him to attack. I'll destroy him.

He pulls from my reach, his lips a thin line as he spews hatred at me. "You want her for yourself? So why didn't you claim her? She smells of heat, her slick so sweet on the air."

He's antagonizing me. I see it in the way his mouth quirks, but I won't fall for it this time. He's manipulative, and everything he does comes with motivation. There is no way Meira just happened to escape from the plane by accident. We have protocols that have never been broken before.

"You know what I think? You made it easy for Meira to run away when you weren't looking so you had a reason to stay with the X-Clan, knowing I'd scramble to find a replacement female for Ander. You counted on me doing anything to save our trade agreement. All the while, you set up your little plan to steal the serum. This wasn't an opportunity you stumbled on, was it?"

There is no other way to explain how Meira never made it to Ander. I've been wracking my brain over this, as our plans are straightforward… females get on the plane and are tied to a chain, end of story. Mihai confirmed he delivered nine women to the aircraft, which can only mean Mad didn't do the one step he was meant to on purpose.

A stoic expression slips over his face, the one he uses when he's lying. Behind him, down in the yard, pack members work tirelessly to bring order back to a chaotic day.

"You've become paranoid, brother," he grumbles, his shoulders bunching up like he's about to transform.

"Were you responsible for the breach in the wall too?" I bellow, anger burrowing into my bones.

He scrunches his nose and scoffs at me like I'm making this up. "You want to blame me for the spread of the virus across the planet, too?"

I'm on him in seconds, my hand on his neck again, and I push him into a backbend over the railing. "There are no such things as coincidences when it comes to you, Stefan. And I can't ignore that we have our first breach on the day you secretly sneak back home."

"Don't fucking call me that!" he snaps, baring his teeth. He loathes that name, as it was my asshole father who gave it to him.

Straining against me, his hands grip my arm for support to avoid tumbling over the balcony. "There was no sneaking inside," he mutters. "What the fuck is wrong with you?"

I can barely control myself as he lies over and over.

"Come on, Dušan. This isn't you. Growing up, we had a goal, remember? Find a way to end the curse. I tried and failed with X-Clan. Shoot me for wanting the best for Ash Wolves. But that bitch, Meira is out there, so let's go hunt her down." There's a glint in his eyes… My stepbrother is a master of deceit. I see this clearly now.

The more he talks about Meira, the more I think about gnashing out his tongue. I don't want her name in his mouth. All I hear are his threats against my fated mate, and that's not going to work.

I wrench him up from his backbend over the railing, and I feel the trembling anger in his body, his wolf growling for release. To my surprise, Mad strains to hold back, the lines on his brow giving him away. His gaze spears over my shoulder. Footsteps close in behind me and I sniff the air, inhaling the earth and wolf scents of my third and fourth.

Lucien and Bardhyl have joined us. Perfect.

Grabbing Mad by the shirt, I swing him around and glance over to the two pack members I trust with my life. I kick Mad's legs out from under him so he drops to his knees before us.

"You're stripped of your fucking title as second to Alpha," I roar. "Your position is at the bottom of the hierarchy in the Ash Pack. Even Betas carry rank over you."

"Fuck you, Dušan. You can't do this! This was my father's pack too. I belong at the top." He starts to get up, but I drive another fist to his face to keep him down, an ache from the strike reverberating up my arm. He groans and stares at me, unflinching.

"About damn time," Lucien growls.

I look up at him. "Lucien, you are now my second-in-command, and Bardhyl, my third. Take care of this turd. I want him chained up in the dungeons."

Bardhyl smirks as he reaches down and grabs Mad by the arm, yanking him to his feet. When Mad swings a punch, Bardhyl laughs and snatches his fist, then twists it behind Mad's back. Mad cries out with pain, and Lucien takes the chance to land a fist into his gut.

I turn away, frustrated to high hell. I just want Mad out of my fucking face. Taking a deep breath, I ground myself and get ready to speak to the pack and put them at ease.

I hate that I'm fuming on the inside at having to imprison my stepbrother when we should have been one team. For once, I want something to go in my favor.

My thoughts swing to Meira and time ticking

away. She's fucking gone! Fury coats my mind. Knots tighten in my gut. She's been gone for a few hours now. The sun's gone down, but I hope she hasn't gone too far. Exhaustion would have worn her out. I think back to when I first found her hiding in the small treehouse she built, living out in the wilderness on her own. She is more comfortable amongst the infected than anyone else. Except she doesn't know these woods in the Shadowlands Sector well. These are my woods, which gives me the upper hand.

CHAPTER 4

MEIRA

My eyes flip open to an explosion of light, and it takes me a few moments of blinking and squinting to find the morning sun blazing right in my direction.

When I move, my legs and ass feel numb and have fallen asleep in the awkward position I ended up in in the tree. I twist around as feeling starts slithering through my legs.

Wait, where's the girl from last night?

I frantically drop my gaze, thinking she fell out of the tree during the night, but I would have heard her. Unless the Shadow Monsters took her swiftly.

Somewhere inside my mind I know she didn't

fall; she must have slipped away from me once I fell asleep. I've been in her position, living in the woods, not trusting a soul. Everyone poses a danger, and she doesn't know me, so why should she trust me?

Still, the notion of her being out there alone curls under my breastbone, and I use my vantage point to search for her. There are trees in every direction, with no animals or birds. I shift to get down from the tree when a horrible, sharp pain floods me so intensely, I shut my eyes and grit my back teeth until the ache passes. The pain from whatever is wrong with me comes more frequent now, like it's building up to something. But I push it aside because I don't have answers right now.

Finally, I jump down from the tree and scan the forest floor around me. Overgrown shrubs smother the land with evergreen vines crawling up the pine trunks. But there's no sign of a body or remains, so I trace my way toward the river. I need a wash, and that's likely where the girl has returned to.

Once there, I kneel and splash the crisp water onto my face, then scrub the back of my neck as well. I take my fill just as a twig snaps from across the river.

I snap my head up and spy a small deer with white spots dotting its back. I'm mesmerized, as it's been so long since I've seen a deer. The little thing has survived this long, and I hope she manages to continue doing so for a long time. When I climb to my feet, she flinches and bursts back into the woods.

I'm up on my feet and turn away from the river. The deer might have been lucky until now, but all our luck runs out eventually. This isn't a world with butterflies and unicorns, but zombies and sex-starved wolves. I hastily rush up the bank and dart into the woods and out of sight so I'm not easily spotted.

But the girl lingers on my mind. Where has she gotten to? As selfish as it sounds, I'd enjoy her company. It sounds strange to think that when I've lived in the woods by myself for years, but if I'm honest with myself, being with the pack was a nice reprieve, even if it was short. Knowing I wasn't alone and that we all worked toward survival in a protected area started growing on me. I sigh at what a hypocrite I am.

My emotions straddle the fence now, when once I couldn't even fathom the idea of joining a pack. It's ridiculous to even have such thoughts, considering how things ended with the Ash Wolves.

I march quickly over the dried foliage and shrubs, my hands swinging by my side as I sweep the woodland for any sign of the young girl. With each inhale I take, I search for distinctive wolf smells and the putrid stench of the Shadow Monsters. My trick to survival has been living next to the undead creatures, as they tend to keep to small herds in the same location. Their presence makes it more likely rogue wolves won't be around to hurt me. It's a simple trick, but it's kept me alive this long.

I keep the river to my right and head straight hoping I'm heading in the right direction to where I used to live in the treehouse. I'll collect what few belongings I have and find a new home where no one will be able to track me.

Step after step, I keep going, needing to forget the Alphas who've affected me in ways that surprise me. It's my fault for letting myself believe I could even have a normal life. The truth stings worse today because I miss them, and I hate myself for having such emotions. I curl my hands into fists against the ache rising through my chest. It's the same sensation as last night… a longing that threatens to rip me apart. With it comes a desperate sensation of leaving behind what belongs to me, but I don't stop walking. I keep pushing, one foot in front of the other.

It's the stupid markings Dušan and Lucien gave me. I sense the prickling over my skin where they bit me, and an unmerciful energy floods me, reminding me constantly I am theirs.

I jerk my focus to the woods, but my head lifts with darker thoughts.

My throat thickens as fear collects into a ball. I could die at any moment if my wolf comes out. But then again, I'm surviving the apocalypse, and death is coming for everyone sooner rather than later. I try to ignore the worry simmering in my mind that I'll be caught. I wrap my arms around my waist, surveying the land with every few steps I take.

Having walked most of the day, the sun is now descending, and with it comes an icy cold. I focus my energy on moving faster through the quiet woods. My weary muscles strain, and I keep going until dusk settles around me. The loose stones on the slanted earth slide under my feet, and I slip, my stomach lurching. I snatch onto a nearby branch and catch myself. Quickly, I hurry down the hill into an open valley where the river roars and foams around the boulders it crashes into.

I kneel at the edge of the water to fill my stomach when I glance over to my side and find the dried-up carcass of a deer, its skin peeled away and rib bones clean of flesh. It looks as though someone tried to find a meal out of the remains.

Near my foot something white glints, and I reach over to the bone that must have once belonged in the animal's leg. It's been snapped in half, but the shattered end sticks out sharply. I tighten my fingers around the bone that fits nicely in my grip.

Sticking it into the waistband of my black leggings, the pointy bit upward to avoid poking a hole through the fabric, I'm up on my feet and heading off quickly again. A small field of wild grass and shrubs surrounds me, the river at my back. I trudge toward the broad oak trees that populate this part of the woods, standing shoulder to shoulder, thick with heavy branches covered in lush green leaves. These lofty guardians will be my home for the night.

Under the protective shadows of the woods, I

search for the perfect tree to scale and settle into, preferably one that has multiple branches crossing. But my attention snags on a rose-red fruit hanging from a tree several feet away.

My mouth salivates instantly as I rush to the plum tree, branches heavily ladened with bright red globes. A cry of joy falls from my mouth, and I jump up and snatch a fruit from the branch. The skin is smooth under my fingers, and I take a big bite, the crisp skin breaking between my teeth with a satisfying snap. Sugary-sweet juices burst in my mouth and drip down my chin. I moan with contentment and finish the fruit in three more bites before I grab two more.

Tossing the seeds to the ground, I help myself to more, unsure how many I've eaten when I finally stop. Juice runs down my fingers, and I wipe them down my pants before collecting half a dozen more to take up into a tree with me.

Mama and I would go fruit picking all the time. She'd stand watch for Shadow Monsters while I scaled trees and threw the fruit down. If we'd known then that I was immune to the undead, it might have made more sense for me to keep guard, especially after Mama had a few close calls.

I miss her terribly, miss hearing her voice, miss

her mixed fruit pies. Cradling my plums, I resume my search for the best tree to settle in when a sudden excruciating sharpness digs into my whole body. I shudder, the fruit tumbling out of my grasp and plonking to the ground as my knees buckle.

The ache pulses, and I hold myself tight, riding the pain that shudders through me like broken glass. My lungs tighten and I'm coughing, spitting blood onto the ground. Just as I did back at the Ash Wolves fortress. Something's really wrong with me. These attacks are coming more frequently, and I don't feel like myself.

I stare at the blood splattered on the dried leaves. This is a recent thing—spewing up blood. I wipe my mouth, my hand shaking as fear slides into my thoughts.

My wolf refuses to come out. I'm broken. But as much as I run away from the safety of the pack and know that wolf could rip out of me at any time, which will kill me if my Alphas aren't near, I don't want to die.

I live at the end of the world and tell myself every day that death could come any moment now, but when I face it head on, feeling it clawing inside me, my bravery fades.

Tears blur my vision and I hiccup a strangled

cry, the throb curling around my heart. All I can think about are my Alphas and how crawling into their arms would ease the ache. My emotions don't even make sense, yet I sit in the middle of a darkening forest on my own and wonder if I've made the right decision.

I cry in my hands because I didn't run away for me. I did it to protect them from me. No matter what I tell myself, that's the fucking truth. I am a danger to them, but on the inside, I'm dying to be with my wolves.

My chin trembles as tears slide down my cheeks.

I'm tired of the constant fear and stress, wishing I could have been born a normal Omega. I remember the female wolf I met on my first day in the Ash Wolves compound, and her words about mates stick to my mind.

"You're gaining a life partner so you won't be alone anymore. Don't you want that?"

I arrogantly said *no,* that I wanted freedom instead. But now that I can't have Dušan or Lucien, my chest cracks with heartache.

The woods are all I've ever known, yet I've let myself experience something I can never have. And going back is impossible. I abandoned them during the attack because it was my only chance to put distance between us, to keep them safe.

The wind shrills around me as I quietly cry. The mistake is mine… I never should have let myself fall for the wolves, because now I don't know how to get them out of my heart and soul.

CHAPTER 5

MEIRA

A chill hums in the air tonight, pressing in around me, the leaves rustling wildly. I tip my chin up as I get to my feet and wipe my eyes. Mama would always say, *"Fate will happen whether you fight against it or not."*

If my wolf plans to burst out of me tomorrow and kill me, then it will happen regardless, and I can't live worrying. So I exhale, letting out the stress and energy bubbling in me, and collect my plums off the ground. With them in hand, I hurry through the forest. The light is fading fast, and I scan every tree I pass for a possible place to sleep.

Pain shoots through my gut and my back seizes, hitting me so fast, I stumble on my feet. Everything freaking aches, but I always feel better after sleep. I reach a great oak with dozens of thick branches spiking outward, two of them crossing over near the trunk. It's perfect. The only thing that would make it better is if I had a blanket, but I've slept in worse conditions.

But when a shattering scream cuts through the silence, I flinch and drop a plum from my grip. My heart starts pounding as I turn and scan the forest. When the sound returns, I can tell it's definitely female and is coming from deeper in the woods behind me. My thoughts fling to the young girl from last night, and bile rises to my throat.

Is it her?

A third shriek comes, and I drop all my fruit to the ground before seizing the sharpened bone in my waistband.

"Hell," I murmur under my breath, because despite what I did for the girl last night, I'm not a hero. I hide and survive. That's what I've done all my life.

I've run away. I've stayed away, but I can't do that any longer. Something in me has changed, and I'm already running through the woods in the direction of the screams. Fading streams of light guide my path. I cut around trees and leap over shrubs, unsure what to expect, but there's only one way to find out.

Another cry echoes around me, louder this time, so I'm getting closer. Trees crowd around me, and my only saving grace is the rustling leaves, covering my thumping footsteps on dried foliage.

I'm running, but the screams don't come again, and a shiver zips up my spine at the thought that I'm too late. That I should have run faster, or maybe I've gone in the wrong direction. I sniff the air, but all I inhale are the smells of timber and soil. My senses have never been as strong as the wolves'.

I want to call out to her, but that's just foolish.

In an instant, someone slams into my back with such speed, and I'm tossed off my feet.

It's me who screams this time, out of pure shock. Sharp rocks scrape my hands and knees, then I collapse flat on my face into the dirt. I push myself up, gritting soil between my teeth and spitting it out.

A dark shadow looms over me, the sudden movement smothering my earlier bravery. I scramble to get up, but I only get as far as to my knees before the wolf prowls closer, moving silently and with deadly intent.

Pale eyes lock on me, wisps of hot breath curling up from lips peeled back over razor-sharp teeth.

Black as the night, this wolf is enormous, fur shaggy and knotted. Half his ear was torn off long ago and has healed to sit upright, not flat against his head like the other. The Carpathian Mountains fall under Dušan's jurisdiction, and for any other wolves to move in, they'd need to challenge him first. So this can only be a rogue shifter.

"Get the fuck away from me," I snarl with a powerful voice. Facing a wolf with fear only gets you killed faster. But what I really need is a distraction, because monsters like him don't walk away from a free meal or a female to rut just because of a strong demeanor. My fingers remain tight around the weapon I grip by my side, a shiver trailing up my legs.

A whimper comes from farther to my right.

The beast turns his head in that direction for a split second. That's all I need… a sliver of time.

I scramble to my feet, energy bleeding through me, and I lunge at the creature.

I slam into his side just as he snaps his head around, and I plunge my sharpened blade into his back, tearing flesh, blood bubbling. Quickly, I wrench it out to strike again, adrenaline propelling me to keep going. To fight and never give up.

But it all happens too fast. His thundering snarls fill the night as he swings around before I can stab him again. Huge jaws snap at my side. I flinch out of the way, then throw myself over his body and into a forward roll before leaping to my feet and running.

I'm trembling, running on adrenaline and terror, the bone slick with blood in my hand. I turn my head quickly to look back. The wolf chases after me, his eyes narrowing with hatred.

I don't stop sprinting. My skin crawls, and I've never moved so fast.

His paws hit the earth, and he growls at my back. This time, I scream. Stuffing the weapon into the back of my pants, I frantically leap up into the closest tree, my hands grasping the lowest branch. I swing my legs up as the air swooshes under me with the ferocity of the beast's attack, but he misses.

I scramble up like a mad squirrel, my hands scraping raw against the bark, branches cutting into my knees, but I can't stop or I'll die.

Suddenly, flesh and fabric tear across the back of one calf. I bellow and lose my grip on the tree, arms and legs whipping about as my heart lunges to the back of my throat. All I can picture is the wolf destroying me the moment I land, and I'm shuddering all the way down to my bones.

Thump.

I strike the ground hard, my back taking the brunt of the pain, and my cries fill my ears.

A shadow hovers over me, the threatening growl stealing all sounds. Fury ripples off him in waves. But I'm on the move, rolling away and scrambling on hands and knees.

Teeth latch around my leg, slicing into my flesh further.

I yell, my back arching, and I shove myself onto my hip, kicking him in the face with my other foot. My hand grabs for my weapon, and I raise it high then drive the sharp end of the bone into his face, right into an eye. The weapon sinks in with a sloshing sound. I shove it all the way in, trying to hit his fucking brain.

He jerks backward, releasing me, and convulses as he shakes his head madly, blood pouring out. The sounds he makes are horrible.

I push myself away and grab onto the tree, dragging myself to my feet.

The wolf is shifting, and in moments, he's turned into a massive man, crumbled off his feet.

Short, black hair sits messily around his square face. He has thick thighs and too much hair across his body. He's yelling with agony as he tugs at the weapon. But I can't bear to look and instead dart to where the girl's cries came from.

I stumble upon her several trees away, and it's the same young girl from last night. My heart bleeds to see the gash across her neck, her lip busted, and her top ripped down her front, revealing her tiny chest. Her hands are tied by a rope around the tree at her back. Her head is down, and she's crying hysterically.

She flinches as I lunge toward her.

"It's only me."

Tears drench her cheeks, and I rush to untie her, constantly looking up in case that bastard comes charging back. My fingers shake as I tug at the knots. I get them loose in seconds, then I rush to the girl who is sitting down and pull her to her feet. "We need to run. Remember what I said last night, swift and silent. Keep repeating that as we get out of here. Stay with me, and please don't run away this time."

She doesn't say a word, just hugs herself with an arm and nods.

I hold her wrist, and we're on the move through the woods, me limping from my calf. It will heal soon enough. My ears prick for any sounds, my eyes sweeping left and right. I spot the rogue wolf in the distance, lying on his side in human form, his body twisted, his mouth parted. The bone still sticks out of his eye. I guess I struck his brain after all. Fucking asshole… He deserved that, and not a sliver of guilt fills me. He isn't my first kill, and if I intend to survive, he won't be my last.

By the time we stop to rest, I have no idea how far we've gone. We're heaving for breath, and that's when I see she has blood over her chin and chest from her busted lip. And my hands are red from the attack. I feel it rolling down the side of my face too, and I hastily wipe it away with my shoulder.

A river gurgles nearby, so I take her hand. "He's not going to hurt us anymore. But we need to clean off the blood before the infected track the smells to us. Okay?"

She remains glued to my side this time and nods, so I guide her out of the woods, where the last streaks of daylight cling to the world.

Scanning the small open area with the river, I find there's no one else around. So we rush over and crouch near its bank, then begin washing ourselves. The rushing sound of the river floods my ears, the water icy against my skin. It's a deeper, greener color in the darkening light. I stare at my reflection, at the wildness of my dark hair and how much longer it hangs than I remember. It easily reaches down past my chest now. Dirt mars my cheeks and brow, but I'm caught in how pale my bronze eyes have become. Thick lashes crown them, and when I look into them, all I see is my wolf peering out at me. *Why won't you come out?*

I glance over to the young girl as she washes herself. "I'm Meira. What's your name?" I ask as I scrub the blood off my hands. Then I sit on my ass and check the damage on my bitten leg. I hiss as I peel back the torn fabric that sticks with blood, hating how close I got to that dickhead killing me.

"Here, let me do that," the girl offers. "I'm Jae," she answers while she pushes the fabric of my leggings to my knee and starts washing my wound with fresh water. It stings, and I bite down on my lip to bear the ache.

"It doesn't look too bad. Think you'll live." She grins at me, and already I like her. Anyone who makes a joke after almost being rutted by a freaking wild man is my type of friend.

I reach down and rip a strip of material from my pants. It's a bit of a strain, as my arms are trembling with exhaustion, but I need to stop the bleeding. I use the fabric to tie up the fang marks that sit around my calf muscle, wrapping it tightly. "So, Jae, how have you survived this long on your own?"

"I'm not alone," she answers quickly, her voice light and almost chipmunk-like. It's a strange comparison, but it's the first thing that comes to mind. Maybe it's her cute, round cheeks and tiny nose. She has a heavy smattering of freckles over her nose and cheeks, and her dark bronze hair has been cut super short. She looks adorable.

"Is your family around?" I ask.

"My sisters are looking for me. We've heard about a place up in northern Romania where there are no undead."

"But there'll be rogue wolves like that asshole back in the woods."

"I know. I just got separated from my sisters, and they have my knife. But we have a place to meet again we agreed on if we ever get lost, and I'm not too far. Thank you for helping me."

"Want me to take you there?" My mind is buzzing with a possible chance to encounter others like me. Omega or Beta, I can't tell what Jae is, but the idea of being in my own small group of females is exciting. No Alpha bullshit to deal with.

"No, it's okay," she responds in a clipped tone, turning back to the river to wash her hands.

I don't push the topic. I understand that in this world, the easiest way to survive is to not trust anyone. And as much as my throat tightens at the rejection, I swing my gaze to the woods behind us and turn my thoughts to the both of us getting up in a tree before nightfall. I'm no fool and suspect she won't be there when I wake up in the morning, but I accept that. In her shoes, I'd do the same.

She's on her feet, and I then remind myself it's best she doesn't want me to help her further. I'm a danger to anyone I'm near, and the last thing she and her sisters need is a ticking time bomb.

CHAPTER 6

DUŠAN

The crisp scent of the wood fills my senses. Everything from the pines to the soil and even the decomposing dead rabbit somewhere to my right.

I sniff the air, searching for the sweet, slick scent of my mate.

But I pick up on not a damn thing, and the sinking sensation falls deeper through me.

I turn and head right because I've been tracking a dead trail for the past few hours. We left our compound just as night settled over the land, splitting up and running in three different directions. We're in human form, but we still have the advantage of our wolves' sharp senses, so we use our noses to try to catch Meira's scent in the dark woods.

I'm hoping the new direction I'm going in brings me across a path Meira has traveled.

Time passes too fucking slow, searching and not finding a single clue. Back in the fortress, Mad is locked up, and my chief of the guards has stepped up and will work on implementing routine as soon as possible. Order helps people get back into their lives and deal with disaster.

I announced to my pack they are now safe, and I will be implementing further security measures to ensure a breach never happens again. And that comes in the form of deciding what I'll do with my step-brother. I can't trust him any longer. That was my mistake before, and he may deny being responsible for letting in the undead, but everything points to him. And to be on the safe side, I locked up Mihai and Cassian, who both had dealings with Mad during the transport of the women to the X-Clan. Right now, I don't have the luxury of time to interrogate them for the truth, so that will have to wait until I return. I can't take any risks while I'm away from the pack.

Finding Meira comes first, and everything else must be placed on hold until I find her. I can't lose her. A piercing fear pinches in my chest that I am too late. That I waited too long before I began the search.

A growl thunders in my chest out of pure frustration. My boots slap the ground with each step I take.

It isn't long before I pick up the decrepit stench of the undead, the smell choking me. I gag, but I swing toward the scent and not away. Meira isn't foolish, and she knows among the undead she is safer from other wolves. It would be my strategy as well.

My ears prick up at everything because I'm alone, and being cornered by those things would be my undoing. But for Meira, I'll risk it all.

The air grows thicker with their decay, and I slow my pace now, making no sound.

I reach to my belt and draw a blade, my fingers curling tightly around the hilt.

There's movement ahead… I count four shadows stumbling through the woods. Bile rushes up my throat, and I hold still. There are no other noises from around me, so is it just them?

A ferocious snarl cuts through the night, deep and guttural, full of menace and warning. I lift my chin and sniff the air, and the familiar musky, wet dog scent that belongs to Lucien hits me. *Fuck, yeah!*

I'm moving before I even make the decision to, darting around trees, keeping my eyes on the undead. Listening… listening… listening.

Footsteps from my right. I pivot and lunge in that direction, rushing past the filthy undead. Where there are a few, more linger. These things tend to move in herds most of the time.

My heart races as I sprint through the dark, slivers of moonlight lighting the way. I grip the knife in my hand tighter.

Another growl shatters the silence. I hurry, my wolf shoving against my insides, demanding release to tear these fuckers apart. To cover distance quicker. Except I need to know what I'm dealing with first.

A figure slams into a tree only a few feet from me.

I freeze and don't make a sound.

Moans come from the creature slumped to the ground, but already it starts pushing back to its feet.

With my heart beating, I lunge in its direction, my knife raised, and I plunge the blade right into an eye, driving it into the brain. Quickest way to eliminate these things.

It drops back down, and I wrench my weapon free, the action making a squelching noise. I wipe the blood on the torn fabric that hangs off its shoulder as I scan the woods up ahead.

Four undead approach Lucien in a semi-circle, and there are more in the woods on their way here. I tense up. All it will take is one mistake, one slip, and they'll be on him. Then more and more will come until it'll be too late to escape.

I whistle low and sharp to catch Lucien's attention. Moonlight glints off the two blades he grips.

He barks out a laugh. "Took you long enough to get here," he teases. "You're getting slow." But I hear the shakiness in his voice. Being out here alone is never a good idea.

"Four more coming this way," I say. "You take the two on your right. I'll take these two."

He gives one nod. "A small group is just to my right. They'll be here soon enough. We need to get the fuck out of here."

Then we charge into battle. It's what we've always known, and this is no different than the hundreds of times before. Except his mention of even more of the undead nearby worries me.

They'll come toward the sounds—they'll *rush* toward us.

I kick the back of the legs of one creature. It falls, and I hurl myself onto the second one, locking an arm around its neck as I stab him in the eye. Pulling the weapon out, I turn and jump at the one on its knees, shoving my blade into the back of its neck in an upward motion.

Someone slams into my back. I'm tossed forward, my pulse spiking.

"Ggffff."

The sound is in my ear, frozen hands yanking at my head.

Panic smothers me. I swing back an elbow and buck at the same time. The weight rolls off, and I scramble up, but another crashes into me, and I'm stumbling about as if I'm drunk, trying to twist around.

The deep moan is right in my ear, fingers digging into my flesh.

My wolf flushes against my chest, but I hold him back. To change now would make me an easy target, as I'd be defenseless during the transformation. I kick my leg back, heel connecting with brittle bone as I hear the clear snap.

I shove the undead off me and whip around to

see Lucien leaping at one of his undead, stabbing it over and over in the face with fury.

Two more of them come at me.

I dart around a tree and grab a handful of one of the undead's hair, except it comes free in my hand with some of the skin.

Disgusting creatures.

As it turns toward me, eyes sunken, skin pulled taut over its cheekbones, I slam its decayed head into the tree trunk. Three times for good measure.

It makes gurgling sounds before it drops to its knees, then I spin around and lash out with my knife. The blade cuts through the throat of the last monster. But not all the way.

"You fucking piece of shit." I kick it in the gut and it falls, and I'm there to finish the job in seconds.

I roar and straighten myself to find Lucien wiping his weapons on the grass. "I bloody hate these things," he snarls as he tucks his knives back into the sheaths on his belt. Bodies litter the woodlands around us.

Unintelligible voices come from the woods on the other side of Lucien, and my stomach drops. The small group Lucien mentioned is on the move.

Hastily, I wipe my blade clean and tuck it away.

He slides in alongside me, and we run in the opposite direction.

No words at first, not until we get far enough to not be heard.

We sprint through the woods, but the sounds coming up behind us seem to grow louder.

I look over my shoulder as a swarm of undead rises behind us where we've left the bodies. There have to be at least a hundred of the bastards.

"Hell! Lucien, you said a *small* group."

He snorts a nervous laugh. "Didn't want to scare you."

I cut him a glare but then smirk, because he's always played down any danger. That's how he deals with shit. Tells himself and others it's not so bad, then he doesn't panic when he faces a wall of damn undead.

I'm the opposite and need everything laid out before me.

He draws in a shaky breath as he looks behind us.

We don't stop, knowing that if we get far enough, they won't be able to trace our smell to follow.

I swallow thickly, praying they don't track us.

Meira

As expected, Jae isn't with me in the tree when I wake up in the morning. I'm not surprised she took off, but I really hope she's smart and makes it back to her sisters. Unease settles in my gut. I'm worried that she's walking into more danger, but I can't spend all my time searching for her when I have to get away myself.

I rub the cold out of my arms and glance down below to the quiet forest. My stomach rumbles, and all I can think about are those sweet plums.

I scramble down the tree and return to the fruit, where I gorge until I sate the hunger pains.

The day is new and bright, so the plan is to make as much headway through the Carpathian Mountains as I can. First, I make a quick stop to wash by the river, then relieve myself. But the whole time, my longing for the Alphas burns through me like a storm.

This feeling for them can't last forever, right? If I put enough distance between me and them, maybe the bond between us will fade.

I remain within the woods and avoid the open

land by the river, but I follow its path. I don't remember how long I've walked, but all the plums I carried with me are now eaten, and the sun sits brightly overhead. My fingers are as sticky as honey, so I slide out of the woods and rush to the water for a quick wash.

Something in the knee-length grass catches my attention from farther ahead. It's lying down, unmoving.

My legs stop working, and I don't breathe for a few moments as I squint for a better look.

A wolf? Except that's not how these fiends hunt. They have too much ego and testosterone to ever crouch and hide. They charge like a fucking bull and take what they want.

Long grasses sway in the breeze. The water gurgles and branches behind me rustle in the breeze. But everything else is dead silent.

Might be a killed animal. But when my thoughts fly to Jae, I lunge forward.

I stare down at the figure. She's twisted, lying on her back. My gaze focuses only on her face, because staring at the shredded body, the bones picked clean, repulses me.

Frantically, I search the features, my heart pounding so hard. Dead eyes stare up into the sky.

This isn't Jae.

It's not her.

A sob chokes past my throat because for a moment, I thought I'd stumbled upon her remains. Whoever this is has been dead for a couple of days, judging by the stench and foam slipping out from the corners of her mouth.

I retreat, but the gagging reflex kicks in strong, and I hurl my breakfast. No matter how many deaths I've seen, I can never get used to it, and the sorrow for whoever that was crashes into me like powerful waves.

With fast steps, I leave that place and return to the safety of the shadowy woodland. I bolt and don't stop until my chest aches from exhaustion. Then I press my back to a tree to catch my breath and can't think of anything else but that poor girl. What if she had been one of Jae's sisters?

I know in my heart there's nothing I can do about it. Still, the grief sits heavily over my chest.

When something sounds in the distance, I tilt my head up.

Thump.

My heart thuds inside my ribcage. There's no sign of the river, and I don't know which way I've been running. Where am I?

I'm in the woods, I tell myself, *so there are lots of noises.* Except these are woods of claws and teeth, and anything out of the ordinary is a potential danger.

A muffled scream comes.

It's clear that someone is in trouble. My thoughts strangle on Jae, on the dead body I found, on remembering how I survived this long on my own in the forest.

By keeping to myself and minding my own business.

I draw in a breath of frigid air, and a tingling buzzes at the base of my spine. And that's when I head toward the distress call to investigate. Maybe I no longer want to be that person, the one who turns away when others need help.

The forest here is denser, and the land is populated with more birch trees than pines. The scent of the forest isn't strong, but it's also closer to where I live…. well, at least in the right direction. Though while there's that benefit, it comes with the knowledge that rogue wolves chose this terrain. I never understood why and figured it had something to do with the low branches, making it an easy getaway should they be chased by the undead.

My body rattles the more ground I cover, convinced this is where the sounds came from. Somewhere in this vicinity... Taking short, sharp breaths, I slow down and dart from one tree to the next.

Cautious, I slowly make progress, but when I find nothing out of the ordinary, I start to backtrack.

A groaning sound comes from just ahead. I slide in behind a tree and peer out from behind it, studying the evergreens and shrubs. That's when one patch of land catches my attention farther away. It's flatter, darker than the rest.

I know right away what it is... a trap that rogue wolves use to capture animals or females. That's how those fuckheads capture women to rut.

And that knowledge alone raises the hairs on my nape. They're around here, but something—or someone—got caught in the trap.

I move quickly before I can think about it too much. From the edge of the deep hole in the ground, I can see that someone down is there, but the shadows make it too hard to see much else. It's definitely not an animal.

"Jae?" The word slips past my lips, and I curse myself for not thinking before speaking out aloud.

"Meira!" a male voice responds.

I freeze and stare intently into the hole as Bardhyl, of all people, steps out of the shadows.

"What the hell are you doing here?" I blurt out. This is horribly bad. If a rogue wolf comes along now, he'll kill this Alpha.

"What do you think, angel legs?" he answers with that Norse accent, and all I see are those deep green eyes staring up at me. There are gashes in the side of the hole where the earth came away from when he tried to climb out.

"I don't need you to come after me, you know. Are Dušan and Lucien nearby too?"

"Never mind that. Be a good girl and get me out!" I hear the panic in his voice. He knows as well as I do that he's in a shitty situation.

I nod. "Be back in a sec." I turn and scan the area for something long and sturdy. I find a fallen log. It's not too broad, but it's freaking long. And he needs something sturdy to climb up.

I run over to the log and snatch the end closest to the hole. Hands wrapped around the rough trunk, I tug, but it barely budges.

Shit, shit, shit.

I can't believe Bardhyl is even here... How did he track me so accurately? Did Dušan send him after me while he stayed with the pack? Well, if I intend to keep that distance from the pack, then this is my chance to just hightail it out of here.

That thought alone sends a twinge of despair through me.

Fuck. My own body betrays me. Okay, fine. I'll get him out, then I'll bolt out of here.

Sucking in a deep breath, I pick up the trunk and heave it once again. It shifts and I shuffle backward, dragging it with me.

If I break my back carting this log, Bardhyl owes me everything.

My heart flutters each time I keep thinking back to his green eyes and that white-blond hair draping over his rounded shoulders.

I hate to admit it, but seeing him has awakened something inside me. Butterflies, mainly. The pesky things flutter frantically in my stomach.

Pulling the log, I jerk it over the ground a bit at a time until I reach the hole, then I dump it down and breathe heavily. Sweat drips down my spine, and I glance down at Bardhyl.

"How are you doing there, baby cheeks?" he asks.

"I don't even know why I'm helping you since

the last time I saw you, you manhandled me. Then you shoved me into someone's house."

He chuckles at me, and as much as he infuriates me, gods have mercy, that is the most delicious sound I've ever heard.

"I can indulge you all you want when I get out. Now stop wasting time."

I huff and turn back to the log that has my muscles trembling. I move to the other end of the dead log, which is close to twenty feet long, and try to work out how to do this.

Bending over, I lift the end up and push it onward. Slowly, the timber shifts over the edge of the hole. I push it, straining in the process, and sluggishly lift my end higher so the base goes into the hole at a descent. It slides forward, and suddenly the base slams into the inside wall and sits there, jammed.

"Crap!" I run toward Bardhyl, gasping for air. "Can you jump up to grab it?"

He arches a brow as if I've asked him to jump to the moon. "Did you get the longest log in the forest?"

"Excuse me? I'm trying," I huff and turn back around. I loop an arm around the log about halfway and heave it backward a bit, then use every inch of strength to lift my end higher.

Sweat rolls down the side of my face, and exhaustion coils right in my chest. I don't know how much longer I can do this before I pass out.

A sudden blur comes from my left.

It slams into me, wiping me clear off my feet, the log falling from my grip.

I scream. My back hits the ground so hard, all the air from my lungs escapes.

Panic strangles my chest, and adrenaline kicks in as a burly form straddles me.

A meaty hand strikes me on the cheek. Stars dance behind my eyelids as pain shoots across my face, and my screams never cease.

I throw punches and thrust against the rogue wolf shifter, who's ripping at my clothes.

He growls, and an overpowering stink of wolf and earth collides into me. I frantically swing my fists into him, never stopping. But it seems to make no difference to this rock of a man.

He's not massive, but he's so fucking strong, it terrifies me.

"Woman," he snarls in my face, like somehow he's forgotten how to speak because he's become the animal he is known for.

Boldly, I rake my fingernails across his face, breaking skin and making him bleed. He hits me in the face again, but I won't stop. I won't ever go down like this.

I pat the ground around me.

My hand latches onto a branch. I snatch it and drive it into his face, hitting him square in the eyes.

The asshole squeals like a banshee and jerks back, clasping his face. I shove against his chest and use that exact moment to slip out from under him.

Scrambling around, I push myself up from my hands and knees.

A strong hand seizes my ankle and yanks me backward. A foot pushes down on my ass, flattening me onto my stomach.

I yell and writhe to escape.

He's tugging on my pants to drag them down my ass.

My terrified screams strangle me. I snatch the first rock I find nearby, then I twist just as his weight vanishes off me.

In a rush, I roll over onto my back, shuffling backward, my hand clutching tightly around the rock. I'm shaking hard, my heart a machine gun shooting off rounds.

Before me stands Bardhyl, as tall and broad as a bear. He towers over the rogue wolf and shoves his fist into the man's face over and over, blood splashing from the deathly hits.

My hero's face twists into fury as he snatches the man's neck, fingers digging into his throat.

The rogue wolf's eyes bug out with terror.

Bardhyl rips his throat out, holding the thing in his grasp.

There's blood and sinew everywhere.

My stomach twists in on itself.

The man drops to the ground, gurgling, bleeding to death, and his end comes swiftly.

Bardhyl tosses the throat aside and spits before wiping his mouth with the sleeve of his coat. More dots splash over his cheeks, and when he looks at me, the hardness in his expression eases.

"Are you hurt?" He leans over and takes my arm, pulling me to my feet, and my hands instinctively reach up against the hard muscles of his chest. He studies me from head to toe, checking for wounds, I guess.

"What you just did was…" I swallow hard.

"That fuck deserved a million times worse for touching you."

"It was incredible." I shouldn't find something

so disturbing exhilarating. But this Viking wolf saved me, and watching him destroy the freak made my heart sprint. He did that for *me*. I ought to hate myself for enjoying such a show, but I don't. My body buzzes when I stare at him, and there's exhilaration from the knowledge that a powerful man is protecting me.

I glance over to the hole, where the log sticks out.

Bardhyl's arm slides across my back, and he draws me close to him. "We need to go now, because more are coming."

Hastily, we leave behind the chaos, and only as the adrenaline starts to fade from my body do I feel the aches and the fear as I realize with stunning clarity that I was almost raped. I push the thought far away because I can't permit those emotions in. I got away, and that's what matters.

When I look over to Bardhyl, my heart pleads with me to return with him back to the Ash Wolves.

Except in my mind, I know the truth that if I join him, I'll bring them death. Returning is not an option.

CHAPTER 7

BARDHYL

My wolf has always felt a connection with Meira, beginning with our very first meeting back at the pack home. I caught her trying to escape, resisting me from the onset. Hell, that drew me to her instantly. She's a survivor and has been one all of her life, which means she's a little spitfire and doesn't back down. That's how someone exists in this world on their own.

I grew up fighting to see another day, so I can relate to her. My pack up in Denmark was slaughtered by a neighboring pack. I only survived because I'd been out hunting that morning. When I found the destruction, I lost myself.

I run a hand through my hair, my fingers

brushing over the scar on my ear from the battle that came afterward.

Revenge turns the most controlled warrior into a Berserker. For weeks, months, I hunted down the Alphas responsible, not caring for my own life. I saw red, burned up with fury, until I caught them.

I heave a loud exhale at the memory. Only Dušan knows the truth of what happened, of the massacre in my wake. He's witnessed the real monster that lives inside me. He had arrived to talk to those Alphas after they betrayed him, and they turned on him.

Yeah, I like to think my interference saved him, but in truth, I lost control and butchered all the Alphas in that pack. Dušan saved me before I could do something worse that I'd never come back from.

My stomach clenches because, after all this time, I like to think that person isn't me anymore.

Shit, I hate remembering those times. I loathe myself for what I was back then.

Meira presses up against me, distracting me. This small Omega has stirred up so much dust in her wake since arriving at our compound.

The majority of the Omegas I've met are passive, and right now Meira is behaving more like other Omegas than she usually does. A typical Omega accepts her role to mate with an Alpha and be his. The union brings enormous pleasure to both but also alleviates the growing aches an Omega goes through if she doesn't get her fill of an Alpha. Quite literally.

But this little fire starter has me all wound up tight and making me feel so much more than I have with any Omega before. I've crossed paths with many, fucked them, but meeting that perfect one hasn't been my fate.

Now, when I look down at Meira holding on to my arm, a monstrous protective nature crashes into me. I'd fight through hell and back to keep her safe.

Except she's taken… Well, spoken for by my True Alpha, Dušan, as well as Lucien. Though this little woman is a complicated mystery because she still hasn't transformed into her wolf. That means the union with her mates isn't complete. That makes her body still release a pheromone that draws males to claim her, to take their chance that they might be her mate.

From what I feel deep in my chest, I worry that my heart is expecting something that won't happen.

I'm not her mate. I can't be, and what I feel is purely a result of her out-of-control pheromones.

"You sure you are all right?" I ask, as she hasn't insulted me in a short while.

She nods and quickly wipes at her eyes.

"I won't let you out of my sight again," I say. "I promise to keep you safe, but you will do as I tell you and not run off, understand?"

"Do you know where the river is?" She ignores me and looks up at me with huge bronze eyes that remind me of a russet sunset. Her features are delicate, and yet there is always fire behind her gaze. Even now, it burns brightly.

"It's not far. I'll take you there. It's on the way back home."

I feel her stiffen beside me, but I say nothing more of it. She is magnificent in every way. She's not mine, no matter how much my craving intensifies for her. But despite having two Alphas who've already marked her, she is ready to run again. I see it in her downward gaze, feel it in her escalating pulse.

She's wild and has no idea what being an Omega means.

"You were never taught the roles of wolves in packs?" I ask, gaining myself a glare.

"I know plenty enough," she remarks. "Alphas are at the top of the food chain and Omegas are meant to be subservient to them. Is that about right?"

I snort a laugh at her feistiness. "Once an Alpha meets his Omega fated mate, he would do anything for her, fight an army, bring her the rarest berries from the deadliest area if she asked. Don't you see? Omegas are the ones who control the Alphas."

She doesn't respond, but the surprise in her eyes says everything. I hope this helps her start to understand how crucial her partnering in a pack is.

We travel without talking, my attention and senses on the forest surrounding us. Danger is everywhere, and I need to get her out of here.

She finally breaks the silence. "Did they send you alone to find me?"

"Dušan and Lucien are also searching for you. I picked up your scent a little way back and was tracking you until I stepped into that damn trap." I should have seen it coming, but I was on the run from a group of undead and wasn't paying attention.

"I can't return with you," she explains casually, like I have no say in the matter.

She makes me want to laugh at how adorable she is to think she stands any chance of getting away from me now that I've found her.

"And I won't stop hunting you down."

She cuts me a threatening glare. Boldly, she peels away from me. We move quietly through the dense forest, over shrubs and under branches. Occasionally, I glance over to Meira, who seems miles away with her thoughts.

"Why did you run?" I ask. There's so much more I want to tell her, but I won't discuss her sickness while we're rushing through the woods.

"I'm sure you're aware of why or you wouldn't be out here. Dušan would have told you everything."

"Running away isn't the answer."

"It is to me. And you've wasted your time. I appreciate you helping me. I owe you everything for that, but I won't go back."

I don't push the topic, as I suspect she will change her mind once she's in Dušan's and Lucien's company. After an Alpha marks an Omega, the connection between them is unbreakable. Even if she hasn't closed the connection yet, the allure of their initial mating has fused their fates together.

The gurgling river comes into view beyond the treeline, and seeing it brings me warmth. If we follow this, it will bring us directly to the Ash Wolves compound.

What I wouldn't give to be back home and have a hearty meal then a sweet minx in my bed. I look over to Meira, who marches alongside me. She's small but has all the curves a man could want. This woman is goddamn beautiful, and the idea of her locked in my room with me sends a twitch through my cock. The more I look at her, the more I can't stop my mind from wandering where it shouldn't. To hear her screams when I bring her to orgasm, to feel her body jerk and shake beneath me.

Shit, those thoughts aren't going to help me keep my distance. I've done well enough on my own this far, and I don't need the complication of an Omega responsibility. Plus, she's already taken.

We carry on to the river in silence. Once there, I scan the area for the undead and wolves, then lift my nose and sniff the air. We're alone. The sun is at noon, so that means we need warmth and food because we won't reach the pack compound tonight.

I toe off my boots as I pull off my shirt, stained

with dirt and blood. When I tug at my belt, Meira clears her throat.

"What are you doing?" she grills me while arching a brow.

I cut her a glance, my grin beaming at the thought of making her squirm. "We're both going to wash ourselves and our clothes. We need to clean the scent of blood from our flesh. Then we'll sit in the sun to dry off a bit."

"Just leave your clothes on then," she retorts, gripping her hips. I adore her aggressiveness. It calls to my wolf, who wants to break her, to dominate her.

"And where would the fun be in that?" I say.

The hitch in her breath makes me smile as I tug down my pants and step out of them. I'm naked. Meira's cheeks are blushing, and despite her stiffness, her eyes dip to my cock. It's half-erect, and judging by her gaping mouth, she's impressed.

I laugh at her inability to hold back. "Your turn, cupcake."

She scoffs and rolls her eyes at me, backing away. "In your dreams."

Giving in doesn't work with me, so I close the distance between us, invading her personal space.

She frowns and tries to retreat, but I grab her arm before she takes off.

"We can do this one of two ways. You strip, or I strip you."

"Get off me. I'm going to wash with my clothes on."

"That's not an option. You won't wash properly, and drying will take longer." I reach for her top, but she slaps my hand away.

Fire flares in my chest, and I snatch her jaw, forcing her to face me. I'm not used to Omegas fighting back, but this wolf pushes and pushes me.

"Have you made a decision?" I say through my gritted teeth, leaning down closer to her.

"I'll do it myself," she hisses back at me.

I release her. "Good."

She huffs, and I watch the fury cross her face, but she doesn't say anything else. Instead, she starts undressing.

I look up ahead to give her some privacy, but she remains in my peripheral vision. Next thing I know, she strolls right past me, bare as a baby, and my attention falls to her perfect ass, moving with each step in a way that hardens my cock.

She steps into the water and looks back at me

over her shoulder, her delicious, pouty lips parting with a smirk. "Are you happy now?"

My lips split into a tight smile. "I can think of a few things that would make me happier."

Meira sucks in a deep breath and jerks back into the water. My eyes latch onto her tiny waist and the curve of her ass, and all I can think about is how much I want those toned legs wrapped around me. The water moves gently, lapping against her hips, and she keeps going deeper.

I join her, the water fucking freezing when I step into it. *Goddammit.*

She turns to me as she dips into the water that now reaches her neck, and the pale bronze orbs of her eyes study all of me. So I march forward, despite feeling like I'm about to pass out from hypothermia. My balls are going to shrivel up to peanuts.

"Are you struggling?" she mocks, the challenge clear on her face.

Accepted.

I dive straight in, not giving a shit that it feels like I've crashed into a tub of ice. I glide underneath the surface, the water murky, but I spot her legs up ahead. I burst out of the water inches in front of her.

She's moving backward, splashing like a drowning fish, and loses her footing.

I can't stop laughing, and when she pops back up, she's furious, but all I can focus on are those pretty little tits tipped with deep red cherries, pointy and hard. Blood dives south, and I start to think that maybe this wasn't such a good idea after all.

Quickly, she covers herself with her hands. "Maybe you should focus on cleaning yourself," she instructs. "And maybe make yourself useful and go collect our clothes to scrub clean."

Oh, she is good at testing my patience. Even so, all I can think about is burying my face between her thighs. So I turn and wash my body and face clean of blood and as much of my scent as possible. Then I collect our clothes. She snatches hers out of my hand, and I shake my head because Dušan and Lucien will have their hands full with this Omega.

Now, I just need to keep my hands off her before I make a terrible mistake.

Meira

*B*ardhyl is crazy dominating, just like Dušan and Lucien, which is why we're both naked in the cold river. I see my mistake now… I never should have saved him from that pit. Now he always has one eye on me, and escaping is going to be damn hard. But I'm not blind to the way he studies my body, how his large cock grows harder. Seriously, these three wolves are packed with enough ammunition to impregnate every female in this country. But I can't ignore the desire he rouses within me.

I splash my face, running my fingers through my wet hair. Bardhyl doesn't move far enough from me to help calm my sprinting pulse. I swallow hard, my throat feeling suddenly dry in his company.

A twig snaps behind me. Adrenaline kicks in, and I flinch forward, stupidly pressing myself against him. His cock nestles against my lower stomach, and now I'm blushing ridiculously.

His large hand wraps around my back, drawing me even closer to him as he laughs. "It's just a rabbit, little bird."

I twist my head back around as the brown furball bounces into the woods.

Bardhyl slides a finger under my chin to look at

him, while his hand sits splayed against my lower back, holding me in place against him. His thumb tenderly caresses my back, sending excited shivers up my spine. I feel his erection twitch between us.

"You don't need to be scared."

I stare up into those deep green irises. I may still be shaken, but I'm furious at myself for being so jumpy. It's Bardhyl distracting me that makes me feel so off-kilter. I've survived this long by noticing everything around me. But then again, I never had a delicious man who has me fluttering with heat each time he looks at me. I have to pull myself together, not think about what it would be like to kiss him, or climb him, or…

Maybe it's normal to feel this attracted to these Alphas since my wolf won't come out to play, which in turn has my hormones going haywire. Though what I have noticed is that since finding Bardhyl and being in his company, I haven't felt the agonizing ache for the other Alphas, or even my own sickness.

Inhaling, I wriggle myself out of his grasp and splash away, even though my body trembles with a need to just give in to the desire pumping through my veins.

But I won't let myself fall prey again. I already

suffer from missing the other two Alphas, so what am I thinking? Adding a third one to the mix? *Great idea, Meira.* Why not make myself a harem, while I'm at it?

"Meira," he says, flashing me a sexy grin.

"Yeah?" I wait for him to speak, clueless as to what he's going to say, but I can only imagine it will be something to embarrass me.

"If you're curious, you can touch—"

"Are you kidding me?" I snap back.

"Don't be shy, sweet lips. Many women who meet me want to, and seeing as we are both naked, I give you permission."

My mouth hangs open at his arrogance and directness. I've never had anyone talk to me the way these Alphas do—mostly because I never grew up with Alphas. They're full of smugness and are always propositioning me. And my body betrays me, of course, lighting up in a fiery blaze on the inside at the smallest of touches.

I raise a brow, hardening my expression. "I'm sure you're well versed in touching your own cock."

He bursts out laughing like he's the king of mirth, grasping a hand over his stomach while he enjoys himself.

What the hell is wrong with him?

"I knew you couldn't stop thinking about my cock. And I was talking about you touching my guns." He smiles deviously as he flexes his biceps.

"Sure you were." I splash him with water, drenching his face and chest, but he keeps laughing at his own stupid joke. Seriously, I should have known he was the joker of the Alphas. When he keeps chuckling, I change the topic.

"Are there Vikings in your bloodline?" I ask, staring at this mountain of a man scrubbing his face. The water reaches his waist, his biceps flexing with huge muscles. His chest is easily twice the width of mine, with light hair across powerful pecs. His stomach ripples with more muscles. With his sandy blond hair draping over his shoulders and strong angular cheekbones, he *screams* Viking.

"My ancestors are said to have been Vikings, yes." He lowers his head to look my way, waiting for my reason for asking.

"I'm curious about your wolf," I begin. "There are stories about Berserkers, fierce warriors known for going into a battle in blind rage, howling like wild animals, biting their weapons."

"And you think I lose control when I take my wolf form?"

I shrug. "Do you ever feel that call from the past? Mama once told me the wolf that forms inside us is a creation of our bloodline."

"She was a smart woman, and correct. If my pa still lived, he'd tell you that Berserkers live fiercely in our bloodline." He snorts a laugh, as if he's remembered something about his father.

I can't stop thinking about him calling my mama smart. From what I've seen, most males see women as property, things to be claimed. So for him to say this leaves me curious to understand more about who he really is.

"My pa trusted only those in his pack, which was why he kept a small tribe. But sometimes trust isn't enough to save you from death when the enemy is bigger than you. It's one of the reasons I joined Dušan. He believes in building a large community of wolves to make us all stronger." He smiles at me as though even the sorrowful talk about his father can't bring him down.

"I'm sorry about you losing your father."

He shrugs. "Shit happens when you live in a broken world."

"If there's one thing all the survivors in this world have in common, it's that we've all witnessed the deaths of our loved ones. And that stays with you."

He turns from me abruptly and walks out of the river. "Time to get out," he orders, clearly not liking the direction of our conversation. "Before you turn into a prune."

After he wrings his clothes of water, he kneels on the wild grasses near several large boulders, where he proceeds to place his clothes to dry in the sun.

Still clutching onto my clothes, I climb out, holding them against me as a shield, feeling insecure about walking naked in front of this hunky wolf.

All wolves insist that being naked is normal, but it sure as hell isn't for me. I'm the woman who's never transformed, so nakedness doesn't come so naturally to me.

Bardhyl's eyes are on me. Always on me. I shuffle forward and hastily lay my clothes out to dry on the warm rock, then sit down quicker than I have my entire life. My heart is pounding loudly, and so much of it has to do with how attracted I find myself to this wolf.

He's flexing his muscles again.

I can't help but laugh at him. "Do women really ask if they can touch your muscles?"

"Why does that surprise you?"

"It's not something I would ever do."

"Yeah, but you aren't exactly the typical wolf shifter, either, my cupcake. You grew up living alone out here."

I eye him carefully. "Not sure if that's meant to be a compliment or insult."

"Neither," he confesses, his voice hard. "It's a fact."

I hug my knees tighter to my chest as the long grass sways around us. The sun is warm on my shoulders while I hold his gaze.

He clears his throat. "On a scale of one to ten, how bad would it be if I—"

"Fifty," I respond, smirking at him because the moment he mentions something being bad, it would be horrendously bad, I suspect.

He arches a brow. "I didn't finish."

"Didn't have to. I got the gist to know it involved doing something I wouldn't agree with."

My stomach flutters at the wicked thoughts that play on my mind. Despite myself, I want to know exactly what he was going to propose.

He studies me intently, the corners of his mouth curling upward mischievously. Yep, whatever it was he had in mind, it was dirty. "Do you ever stop being so serious and just enjoy someone's company?"

His question catches me off guard, as it never occurred to me until now that I came across that prickly. But when he looks at me with a raised brow, I can't help myself and say, "And do you never cease joking?"

His expression hardens. "Sweet cheeks, you may not love me if you see who I truly am."

ove! Did Bardhyl just say that four-letter word?

Of course it's a figure of speech and he doesn't mean actual love, but the word sticks with me. Maybe because the only person to ever say it to me was Mama. I've never had anyone to whom I've felt close enough to even joke about it.

Bardhyl makes me want to sit around and talk to him for hours, even if he annoys the hell out of me.

He's lying on the grass now, his eyes closed, enjoying the sun for the short period of time as our clothes dry.

I'm staring out toward the river, my back to the warm rock.

Running away now would be stupid, so I'll bide my time and wait until this big guy next to me is really asleep. Then I'll escape.

I am so tired of always looking over my shoulder. Exhausted of feeling like a rabbit on the run in a world filled with wolves. What I need is to find the biggest colony of Shadow Monsters and move in near them. Sure, they aren't the prettiest sight, and their constant gurgling, moaning sounds are annoying, and they stink, but beggars can't be choosers, right?

And I refuse to give in to my emotions, reminding myself that getting away is for the safety of the Alphas. They'll eventually get over me. They have to… I have to believe that so I know it's possible to do the same.

"It's time we get a move on," Bardhyl orders. "We find shelter for the night, and tomorrow we should reach home." His shadow falls over me as he grabs his clothes from the rock next to me.

I reach up with one hand while still covering my chest with the other and take mine, then hastily drag the top over my head, threading my hands through still-damp sleeves. I could have done without wearing moist clothes.

"You're not my favorite person right now," I say

to him as I wiggle my feet into the pants and drag them up my legs before getting up to quickly cover myself.

"Then I'm doing my job right. I'm not trying to make you like me," he grumbles.

I turn to face him as he buttons up his jeans and partially tucks his shirt in, his head low, blond hair cascading forward. All I can see are strong, powerful arms and muscles. This bulking man towers over me easily, and he'll use force to keep me by his side. For that, I hate him. But my body responds to him in beautiful ways, and a thread of arousal rises inside me, licking over my skin, hinting at a desire for more.

His offhanded commands irk me, though. "I don't expect you to like me, but I'd hope you'd have some compassion. I'm broken, Bardhyl. A danger to the pack. Can't you see that's why I can't return with you?"

I shift to walk away when he reaches over and grabs my jaw, not hard enough to hurt, but enough to keep me locked in his hold. His thumb caresses my cheek, and he gazes at me with such passion, I can't bear to work out where things stand between us. I don't want to know, in truth, because I'm already grieving over leaving two Alphas. So please, universe, don't throw another into the mix. I sense my body responding to Bardhyl in ways it has with Dušan and Lucien. Heat burns between my thighs. The wolf inside me may not have come out yet, but she isn't shy about letting me know which men she craves.

"What do you think is going to happen when you don't return to your Alphas?" he asks.

"What are you talking about?"

All I can focus on is where he touches me and that while I'm under his gaze, somehow I'm the most important person in his world.

Bardhyl reminds me of the other two, and rather than letting myself trip over myself for this wolf, I have to remain strong. Summoning my strength, I tear free from his grasp.

"They will get over me and find someone else. All the females in your pack would love to mate with them." Even as the words leave my mouth, an ache spears over my chest. I've heard of wolves living happily without a mate. Unmatched Omegas make perfect companions to Alphas without that deep-felt connection. It's possible.

Bardhyl shots me a puzzled look, like I've lost my mind. "I think you and I need to have a long conversation about the birds and the wolves."

I laugh. "It's called the birds and the *bees*."

"Not where I come from, and clearly you know very little about your own kind. Or that if you don't return to your Alphas, the ache you feel from your distance will grow so intense that you'll wish you were dead."

No, distance will break our bond. It has to.

With frustration, my response rips out of me. "Scaring me won't make me change my mind. You can twist words into any form you want, but they don't mean something different."

"I never took you for being philosophical. You're the kiss-and-run kind of girl to me."

"Ha. Goes to show how little you know of me." I turn away from him, my insides blazing with anger that he sees me as someone so fickle. I flip him the finger. "Don't mistake my admiration of your naked body earlier for something it's not. I hate you. No matter how big your dick is."

His footfalls fall in behind me, and he's chuckling to himself. I'm cringing on the inside for blurting out the last part. I wanted to insult him, but instead I complimented him. What is wrong with me?

Oh, I know. The vulnerable, sexually deprived side of me has me saying ridiculous things.

"If you want, cherry lips, I can show you later how much bigger it can get if you think *this* is big."

I refuse to give in to him and don't respond. Out here, I carry the upper hand by being immune to the Shadow Monsters, and that is my strength. Now, if we could just run into some undead, all would be dandy again.

Everyone has their own path in life, and mine is to be alone in the woods. I'm not afraid of the dark or the virus. What scares me the most is other people.

Getting too close.

Then losing them.

That heartbreak is worse than death.

After losing everything once, I vowed to never go to war with my heart again.

The far-off memory of my mama faded, and I let it dance away. Now, I keep walking and wait for the right moment to make my own move.

"You smell different," he says out of the blue, and when I glance his way, his eyes focus on me.

"Every wolf has a unique scent," I correct him.

"But yours is more than a wolf smell, Meira."

I pause and raise my chin to him. Something in the pit of my stomach hardens. "What are you saying?"

"That when I inhale the air around you, my wolf goes crazy to claim you, but he also whimpers at the sickness you carry."

My cheeks burn. "I already know. It's my wolf who refuses to come out. But thanks for reminding me how obviously different I am."

"That's not what I'm saying."

He falls behind as I march ahead. But then he's suddenly at my side and snatches my wrist.

"Have you never wondered why you're feeling sick and throwing up blood? Dušan told me how sick you were back at our compound. But no shifter has that kind of illness, even when a wolf hasn't shown itself yet."

"Yeah, so? What do you want me to say? I don't know why I'm fucked up."

"Oh, baby girl." He clasps the sides of my face, but I've had enough of everything, and I shove my hands against his chest.

"Just stop."

"No. I won't until you properly understand."

"What the heck are you talking about?" I'm yelling now, my body trembling. "Don't talk in circles. Tell me what you know."

His expression grows stoic. "Dušan ordered tests of your blood while you were at the compound, and we think we know why you're sick and why the undead don't touch you. It may also be why your wolf won't come out."

My stomach drops right through me. "What did the test show?" My voice comes out lighter than intended, and I hate that there's fear behind my words.

Except a chorus of moans rising from up ahead of us distracts me.

I jerk my attention to a gang of at least twenty Shadow Monsters rushing toward us. We're out in the open, talking too loudly, drawing their attention.

Bardhyl draws me by the hand in the opposite direction, but my mind screams at me to pull away from him and run toward the undead. This is my chance to get rid of this Alpha. To be on my own and hightail it out of the Shadowlands once and for all.

But I can't get his words out of my head. He knows what's wrong with me. Since losing Mama, I've wanted to understand why I'm different. What if Dušan's discovery can provide me with a cure to my wolf being stuck inside me?

I choke on the hope curling in my chest.

"For fuck's sake, Meira, move your ass!"

The undead come fast, and panic twists Bard-hyl's expression, heavy with the dilemma of if he should leave me behind and save himself.

But if we split up now, I'll never know the truth of what is wrong with me.

Goddamn Shadow Monsters. Of all times to attack, they come now?

I spin away from them, and then we run.

Bardhyl holds on to me tightly, as if to keep me safe, but *he* is the real one in danger here. If I want to hear about the blood test, I need to make sure he survives. Funny how irony can be a pain in my freaking ass.

Bardhyl

My breaths come hard. I shove my feet to the ground, covering the ground fast, hauling Meira alongside me.

For those few seconds, I swore she'd take off and use the undead as a mask, but me telling her about her blood test couldn't have come at a better time. I'll use that to keep her by my side for as long as possible and ensure I get her back to the pack.

I dare a glance behind me. Those fucking assholes aren't giving up, though we've put a fair distance between us through the dense woods. They won't stop until they lose sight of us.

"What did the test show?" she asks between gasping breaths. "Tell me."

"Later," I retort.

"No, now. It's the perfect time," she huffs beside me. "What if you die and I never find out?"

She infuriates me. I have a mind to toss her over my lap and make that pretty little ass of hers pink.

I cut her a harsh look, seeing right through her plan. "Then you better make sure I don't die."

She narrows her gaze, and I know that if we weren't running at full tilt, she would have punched me. I might have enjoyed it, too.

I leap over a dead log right after her and swerve to follow the downward slope of the land.

When she twists her head toward me, the smile on her face is cunning and not something I expect. But she doesn't faze me. If she wants to play this game, she won't know what hit her. I can push her buttons if that's how she wants to do this.

The foliage-covered ground rushes out from under my feet, and I crash onto my ass, a grunt rolling over my lips. I scramble back up just as Meira tumbles over the steep descent. I lash out and snatch the back of her top, seizing her against me rather than letting her fall.

She's breathing heavily, and I stare behind us to where a scattering of the undead track after us. The herd has definitely thinned, but even with my blade, I couldn't risk a fight here. Too many followed. What we need is a means to hide and conceal ourselves until they disappear.

"There!" Meira yells out, pointing to something slightly to our right, but all I see are trees.

In moments, we burst out of the woods to a small clearing at the edge of a cliff, spearing outward on either side of us.

My eyes lock on a dilapidated bridge made of ropes and wooden planks that looks like it might crumble if I step foot on it. It spans about a hundred feet over a gorge, to a side that seems free of the undead. But it looks so high, I'm not sure how safe the bridge is.

Meira goes first to cross this rickety thing, which is brave of her.

I smirk to myself, but that moment of cheer

evaporates when a guttural moan comes from behind me.

Quickly, we rush onto the bridge, the wood groaning under my weight, and the whole thing starts swinging from side to side with our fast steps.

I make the mistake of looking down to the snake-like river down below, and my head spins from the distance. I clutch onto the rope, my legs locking in place as I picture myself falling over and plummeting to my death.

I fucking love my life, and I fight tooth and nail every day to survive. But now, I can't get the image of me falling through this broken bridge and dying out of my head.

My heartbeat pounds in my ears.

"Bardhyl, what are you doing? Move your legs," Meira berates me, her voice irritated.

But my eyes are set on the river so far below.

Soft hands touch mine as I hold on to the rope with a death grip.

"Listen to me." She yanks me by the hand. "Look at me. You need to move, and now, or *I* will be the one to push you over the edge."

When I meet her gaze, I believe she means

every damn word. "Is that how you help someone off a ledge?"

"Well, it got you moving, didn't it?"

Only then do I realize I've taken steps forward.

"Don't look down. Seriously," she says. "Just focus on my voice and travel fast. They're right behind us."

I don't look back. I do exactly as she says. I shake all over, one hand holding on to Meira's and the other on the rope. Step after step, we're closing the distance.

With a sudden sway, the whole bridge shifts beneath us. I latch on to the rope harder and look back to find three undead stumbling onto the damn thing. There are half a dozen more on their heels. Will the bridge even take all our weight?

"Hurry up," Meira ushers me. "Let's go. You can do this, Bardhyl."

Focusing on her voice, I do just that. Quickly, I step after her, the bridge swinging, my stomach lurching with each movement. With only a third of the distance left, we start rushing.

My heart slams ferociously in my chest.

Don't look. Don't look the hell down.

Meira pushes ahead of me and is waving me to hurry, and in seconds, I'm alongside her on the other side. I could kiss the damn soil beneath my feet.

I seize the blade from my belt and turn around as the creatures stumble wildly toward us. I lunge to the edges of the rope and in one swipe, I cut the top rope on one side, then I crouch down and draw my blade through the cord tying the bridge to the timber pole near me.

The bridge suddenly collapses on its side, sending the undead hurtling down to their final deaths in the valley. They fall like blobs, smacking into the river and the overgrown banks.

One of the suckers is hanging on to the bridge, while others are still climbing on.

I cut the ropes attached to the stakes on the other side, and the whole thing collapses away, taking with it the last undead.

There's another bridge closer to the pack fortress. Getting home is going to take longer than I want, which fucking sucks.

"Okay, we need to go." I'm on my feet and spin around as I catch Meira going in the opposite direction.

I snatch her wrist and haul her toward me. She spins in my direction, her hands slapping against my chest as we collide. All I see are those eyes, those bronze irises, and I don't know what comes over me, but I'm leaning down and kissing her before I can find my senses.

She freezes at first, taken aback by my kiss. Fuck, I am too, and I start to pull away just as she kisses me back, parting that delicious mouth. Her small hands curl around the back of my neck, pulling me closer, pressing her gorgeous breasts against my chest.

Fuck me!

I shouldn't be doing this. But my cock twitches and I hold her tightly, against my better judgement. It's she who finally pulls away. When I let her go, I'm short of breath, and my head fogs with what I've just done.

"We leave now!" I grab her hand and start marching. My heart hammers in my chest and my dick presses against my jeans. What the fuck is wrong with me? I freak out about dying on the bridge, so my response is to kiss her?

The woods grow denser as we follow the line of the gorge while I try to get my head straight. To remind myself whom Meira belongs to. And it sure as fuck isn't me. No matter how much I want to rip off her clothes and claim her right now, to make her scream my name.

Hell. Those images in my head of me taking her aren't helping. Just need to clear my mind, that's all.

"I'm surprised the big bad and powerful Bardhyl is afraid of heights. I thought you were indestructible," she jokes and half-laughs, but I hear the strain behind her voice. She kissed me back, so I'm not alone in this sudden awkwardness. But if the only way to deal with our mistake is to pretend it didn't happen, then I'll play along.

"Baby cheeks, everyone in this world is flawed, and I never said I was perfect." Case in point, right now I want to swing her in my arms and kiss her, no matter the cost.

I am completely flawed.

CHAPTER 9

DUŠAN

I fucking hate the woods. I never thought I'd admit that, considering I live in the Shadowlands forest, but *fuck!*

"Where the hell can Meira be?" I bark, frustrated to hell.

Meira is nowhere. I've only found these damn undead and a rogue we ran into. Kicked his ass and kept going. With our heightened sense of smell, we ought to have picked up on her scent by now. But that tells me we're going completely the wrong way, even after changing directions several times.

"I bet Bardhyl found her," Lucien murmurs. "He's the luckiest of us. He always wins on card night."

I cut him a glare, but hell, his reasoning might

be more accurate than us wandering aimlessly through the woods. If Bardhyl tracks her first, he'll keep her safe and protect her with his life. But not knowing if that's the case is driving me insane.

A bird chirps somewhere around us, followed by another. There are no other animals. "We follow the river. She would have made stops to drink and wash, so we'll pick up her scent." My initial thought was that she'd gone to high ground, as there are pockets of caves up there, offering protection. Except I'd been mistaken.

"Agreed." Lucien nods and we cover the ground quickly, sticking to the riverbank.

Aside from a few animal prints, the pebbled shore shows no marks. We've walked for a long while when Lucien asks, "What are we going to do with Mad?"

Just thinking about my stepbrother raises the hairs on the back of my neck. I never should have appointed him so highly in my pack or ever trusted him with delivering Omegas to our trade partners.

"He'll have three options. He submits and will be under constant guard, he leaves, or he pisses me off so much I'll kill him." The words taste sour in my mouth, but he's fucked up before and I always give him another chance. The fault is mine for treating him differently than my pack because he's family. But my pack is family too, and I've had enough.

"About time," Lucien snarls. He and Bardhyl have warned me about Mad for years, and I chose not to listen. Well, that shit changes now.

We push on, the surrounding trees swaying in the breeze. It feels like we've walked for hours when Lucien pauses and stares down at the bank. The ground is all torn up, footprints going in and out of the water. I crouch down and trace my finger along the edge of a bare footprint that's too small to be male. The steps are perfectly aligned, no stumbling, meaning this hasn't been made by the undead.

I take a deep inhale of the mud, the freshwater, the sweet grass, and beneath it all is another scent. It's faint, but it carries a wolf signature and that sickly blood smell. It's gone in seconds, but that's all I need.

"She was here." I shoot to my feet, scanning the area for a clue, something.

"Someone was with her," Lucien states, pointing his chin at larger footprints. No shoes, either. "Told ya. Bardhyl got to her."

Thank fuck, if that's the case.

"These barefoot markings have them going into the river on purpose. To wash off blood, perhaps, and stop the undead tracking them. Or they had wolves on their heels and needed to hide their scent."

"The tracks had to be made today. They're still fresh," I say. "We're close." Hope that we might finally find Meira spears through my chest.

We exchange quick glances and head down the river, toward the direction of our pack. It's where Bardhyl would have taken her.

Together we pick up our pace. Lucien and I have been inseparable since we were kids. After losing his mate, he was withdrawn when it came to finding another partner. It didn't stop him from seeking out Omegas to fuck—he never had a lack of females eager to fill his bed—but it's never been anything more than one night.

Until now, with Meira. I should be furious that he touched what belongs to me, but fated mates don't work that way, do they now? Wolves will choose each other irrespective of what the heart wants. Yeah, it fucking burns to picture him taking her.

What choice do I have if the wolves have picked

their mates? I can't lose Meira or my closest friend, so I swallow my damn pride. We'll find a way to make this work.

"Who made the first move, you or Meira?" I can't help myself and want to know.

He doesn't meet my gaze when he responds, knowing too well what I'm asking. "Do you have an issue with us?"

I've always thought one day I'd find my fated mate and it would be just the two of us. But it's rare for my dreams to become reality, as the universe likes to fuck with me.

"Fate has a wicked sense of humor and kicks you in the teeth when you least expect it," I respond.

He throws me a stare from hooded eyes and huffs. "I knew you'd bring this up. I don't need your jealousy crap. I just…" He glances up at the sky. "I don't fucking know. It's just that when I'm with her, the heaviness I've been carrying around with me lifts." He shrugs. "I haven't felt this for a very long time, Dušan. I would never step on your toes, you know that. You're like my brother."

When he meets my gaze again, there's a hardness behind his eyes, like he doesn't know what to make of his feelings. Of how Meira swept into his life and knocked him off his feet without warning. How both our wolves connect with her…

Everything about her should send off alarm bells, but instead I want to take her, strip her down, and claim her over and over. To mark her so many times that her wolf has no choice but to goddamn show itself already.

"What if we lose her to the disease?" Lucien murmurs, as if reading my mind.

"It won't happen." My spine stiffens. "I'll tear the fucking world apart before I lose my fated mate."

Bardhyl

A snap of lightning spears over the darkening sky, quickly followed by a thunderous growl. The earth trembles in response, and the first drops of rain hit my face.

Meira is running alongside me while I scan the area for shelter. Hiding in a tree isn't going to cut it, not with the storm rolling in. When I look across my shoulder to Meira, her gaze is sharp, taking in our surroundings.

Farther to our right, the mountain climbs harshly, a rockface appearing behind the trees. My hand slips into Meira's, and I guide her in that direction. Maybe we'll be lucky and find shelter.

We swerve through the thicket of the woods when the land suddenly ascends severely, rising and rising into the cliffs overhead.

The rain comes down in fat drops, soaking us. My skin pricks with cold, and I draw Meira to my side.

"There," she calls out, dragging me to her left. I spot the darkened hollow in the side of the mountain. Four other caves lay waiting for us, and I'll take any at this moment. I release her hand and hastily pick up small branches and twigs near the trees not yet wet. Wet timber is a bitch to make fire from, so I rush with haste, grabbing an armful. Meira does the same, collecting larger branches covered in leaves. We're soon rushing into the nearest cave with our bundles.

I exhale as cold water drips down my back from my hair. I move in deeper and dump the wood on the ground, then sniff the air for any indication of an animal or the undead being in here. It's pitch black, but all I smell is the stale cave.

I take out the lighter from my pocket. I'm not a caveman; I came prepared. A quick flick and the cave illuminates, revealing a long, narrow area that offers us the chance to be farther from the entrance of the cave.

I get to work and build a small fire in the middle of the cave, giving us plenty of space to sleep behind it.

By the time I finish and kneel in front of the flames, bathing in the heat, Meira has made a makeshift bed of large palm-like leaves layered on the floor.

Outside, the rain pummels the land, coming down in sheets.

"That storm came out of nowhere." Meira joins me by the fire, warming her hands. The orange glow beams over her beautiful face. And this is exactly where I want to be… enjoying the rays of her smile when she glances at me with a question on her pouty lips.

"Food would be amazing right now," she says, and I think she's batting her eyes at me. Does she think that's going to work? I'm not going out there in this weather to search for an impossible meal.

"It would be," I respond. "When you come back with something for us, I'll have a small spit over the fire."

She glowers at me, and I chuckle at how predictable she is sometimes, though I've been with her long enough to know she doesn't typically flirt to get things she wants. Is this a sign that she's growing comfortable in my presence?

"You're not exactly being a gentleman," she answers while sitting down in front of the fire, crossing her legs.

"Never claimed to be one, or a hero, or anything else. I am what you see in front of you. An Alpha following orders and keeping you in check."

She tilts her head in my direction. "Then why did you kiss me?"

"To show you that you're wrong."

She stiffens and folds her arms over her chest. "Excuse me?"

"You think you have everything sorted out and that running away will solve your shit. But nothing in life goes as we expect it, now does it?"

She narrows her eyes, that cute little nose wrinkling.

I push loose strands of hair out of my face. "You

never expected me to kiss you, and now you can't get me out of your mind. I know you can't. It's written all over your face." And it's constantly on my mind, the sweet cherry taste of her lips, her racing breaths, and how she clutched on to me, desperate for more.

"No, it's not. Don't kid yourself," she barks in response.

I laugh, and already I smell her desire on the air, the faint slick, delicious scent that stirs my wolf. It calls to him, and here she tells me she's not thinking about me. Right.

I shift toward her, and she responds by scrambling to her feet, backing away.

"Are you afraid that you'll lose control, and when you start, you won't be able to stop?"

"Remember, *you* kissed *me*." She tightens her arms under her chest, pushing up her perky breasts, the dampness of the fabric gluing itself to the curve of those perfect tits. I can't help myself. My cock springs up and twitches in my pants.

I get to my feet. A few quick steps, and I close the distance between us. A warning bellows in my head to back away. That I'll be the one who won't be able to stop.

Except when she looks at me like a mouse

trapped by a lion, the excitement in my veins propels me forward. It has been too long since any woman has made me feel this alive, this addicted, this fucking captivated.

I reach out and snatch the back of her neck, wrenching her toward me. She gasps, that little sound driving me crazy with need. Goddamn, where did this hellcat come from?

I take in her slick smell again, and fuck, she's going to be my undoing. I should have known the first time we met that I would never walk away from this Omega.

And now that I have her in my grasp, I don't know how to pull away.

The unbearable ache in my chest demands we take her as ours. This is the right time, the perfect moment for us.

She looks me in the eyes, challenges me with her stare, having no clue about her place in the wolf world. Maybe that's what attracts me to her so much.

There's so much difference between us that it's refreshing to have an Omega who fights me, who doesn't just do as I order. Most Omegas have lost their fire, accepting their fates. And as such, most just search for an Alpha, desperate to find their matches and fall into their routines. That isn't what I want...

"Are you going to tell me about my blood test results?" she demands.

Lightning steals the shadows around us, the rain drenching the woods outside.

"Here's the thing. I'll make you a deal," I begin, not releasing her from my hold. She shoves her fists into my arm, but I'm not letting her go just yet. "You and I will kiss, and then you will beg me to touch you, to finger that tight little pussy. When we get to that stage, you tell me to stop, and I won't touch you for the rest of the night."

"Are you fucking insane? I'm not agreeing to that." She shoves her hands against my chest, and I release her. She stumbles, her cute breasts bouncing and drawing my attention.

"If you don't tell me to stop, I win. Then you are mine for the night. How does that sound?"

She stiffens, blinking at me blankly. Oh, she's good. "Is that your standard pickup line?"

I look her up and down. "I've never had a woman reject me, if that's what you're implying."

"And if I don't agree to this ludicrous idea?"

"Do you have another suggestion to keep us entertained all night?"

She tilts her head back, her chin high. "Um, sleep."

There's no way I can sleep when all I can think about is our earlier kiss, and I dip my attention to her parted lips. I should back away, but I've let myself go this far, and pulling back is as easy as getting starved wolves to back away from an escaping deer. In other words, it's impossible. Hell, I don't fucking want to pull away from Meira. She's affected me so much, and maybe I just need to get her out of my system.

She makes a humming sound. "So, when I win, you will tell me immediately what my blood tests said, right?"

I lean forward and whisper in her ear. "Sure. But cupcake, you won't be able to resist. I promise you that. You'll be screaming my name well into the night."

CHAPTER 10

MEIRA

I must be insane to even contemplate this. Bardhyl is a freaking horny wolf who sees this as an opportune time. Why can't I get the memory of our kiss out of my head? How I desperately clung to him, needing so much more of him, how I sensed the ache easing while in his arms, just as I did with the other two Alphas.

I sidestep to get away from him, to catch my breath because I'm drowning in my own arousal. When I look at him, a fogginess clouds my judgment. Even now, his smell is all over me—the musky wolf, the freshness of rain on his skin, even the mud on his shoes.

There's no denying it. I've thought of kissing

him since our first encounter at the pack fortress. Then again, I felt that way about Dušan and Lucien. And, well, look where that got me. Now I'm stuck in a cave during a storm with a Viking hunk, and instead of flat-out driving him away, I'm contemplating some crazy game where he turns me on and I have to tell him to stop. Who does that?

"Meira," he calls to me, but I keep my back to him, needing to find some sense of rationality about this situation and for my cheeks to cease burning.

"I don't think this is…" I start, but then he steps close in behind me. The heat of his body pours over me, and I seem to have lost my ability to think.

"What's that, cupcake?"

Inhaling deeply, I reach inside and track down a sliver of common sense, then manage to say, "I vote for sitting by the fire and trying to sleep. Your idea is crazy. We're not doing it."

An ache sits heavily in my lower stomach, just like it did before Lucien and Dušan took me, and now it stirs again. It's my wolf, rising to the occasion.

Maybe for my wolf, I should give this a go. If Bardhyl's presence awakens her, I'll regret never attempting to bring her out. I want to laugh out loud at my ridiculous reasoning. As much as part of that is true, I can't get the image of his nakedness by the river out of my head. His large cock, his large hands, his promise of what he'll do to me. His presence alone squeezes my libido.

Maybe some women can push away such a man, and I always thought I'd be the same. Apparently, I'm wrong. I'm just a wolf in heat. My resistance is a thin façade with cracks threading through the surface.

I turn to face him, my chin high, wearing my bravery, which is a terrible mistake. That earlier resistance has crumbled around me.

The moment I lay eyes on him and discover he's just in his jeans, the top button open, I forget my argument. When did he take his shirt off? "That's very presumptuous of you." I eye his Adonis-like chest that leaves me weak. "I haven't agreed to your crazy idea."

"Let me tell you what you're thinking." He reaches over and slides a strand of hair that was caught in my lashes behind an ear, but I bat his hand away. "In your mind, you will slip away from me and never see me again. Yet the idea of finding out the truth about what's in your blood is tempting, isn't it? Should you play my game and gain some information, or forget it because you've lived this long without knowing? What difference would it make, right?"

I narrow my gaze at him.

"You know I'm right."

"And if you are, then you're an asshole for using a piece of important information to get into my pants."

He *tsks* at me. "I said you would be mine for the night. Who said anything about sex?" He smirks evilly. "When I win, you will give me a full body massage all night long."

I roll my eyes hard at him. "You love playing games, don't you? I can see the way your eyes twinkle as you twist everything around your words. But I can tell you now that when we kiss, you will be shocked at how quickly you will lose."

"So that's a *yes* then?" He sticks out his hand to make this official, and I accept because he may be right about my intentions, but I will burn in hell before I let him know he's right. He always brings out the competitive side of me, I've noticed.

He suddenly backs away and stands by the fire

just in his jeans. Even his boots and socks are off. My toes wriggle around in my wet shoes. I follow suit and toe them off before returning to the heat.

"So," I say amid the strange awkwardness, "are we doing this?"

"Whenever you're ready. I always let the woman make the first move so it's clear they want this and I'm not forcing them to do anything against their will."

He stares into the fire as he talks, his hands stretched out, and I'm trying to decipher the expression on his face. He gives nothing away.

"Did you learn that from Dušan?" I ask, remembering my first time with the Alpha and how he pulled away when I hesitated after he went down on me. It had nothing to do with pleasure, because I still shiver at the memory of his tongue on my pussy. It was the fear of what my wolf would do.

But a simple kiss with Bardhyl I can do with my eyes closed. I move toward him, and he doesn't even look my way. He stands so tall and muscular, his nose slightly crooked, which only adds to his attractiveness. Spectacular green eyes that I want to dive into, and long, blond hair tumbling over his shoulders and falling to his chest. But my gaze lingers on his bicep for a bit too long and then shifts over to the tightness of his abs, the way the firelight dances over his perfect body… all sharp angles and cuts. He has to be a Viking god, because how else can one person be so perfect?

But if anyone is not going to be able to say *no*, it will be him. I press closer to him, nudging my breasts against his side on purpose. He swings an arm around me while pivoting his whole body to face me.

Danger and arousal swirl behind his gaze. I push myself against him once more, my hands planted on his hardened pecs that twitch beneath my touch, which he does for show.

"Bardhyl." I breathe his name on a moan. "You are not doing a good job of winning me over."

"Oh, have we started?" He mocks me, and I'm fuming, angry words rolling over my throat, but he turns on me so fast, I lose my voice.

Strong hands grasp my hips and lift me in a heartbeat, just enough to place my feet on his. He smiles wildly as he walks me backward until I hit the wall, and I'm pinned in place by his huge frame. I shouldn't enjoy this, but I love his aggressiveness.

With each inhale, I smell his muskiness, and my body trembles before he even kisses me.

He plants one hand on the wall above my shoulder, and the other strokes my jawline. His eyes devour me, and beneath his stare, I start to feel absolutely tiny in comparison.

"I've been trying to figure you out," he says, his voice dark and raspy

"Yeah, how so?"

"To understand what would make a woman like you happy."

I lift my chin higher. "That's easy. Freedom."

He nods. "I got that part, but I mean sexually. The feistiest of people love to be dominated when it comes to being fucked."

"We can't sleep together. That was part of the rules you made up." I smile cheekily.

"There were no rules about talking about it." He leans in closer, his cheek brushing against mine, his breath heavy on my ear. He doesn't touch me anywhere else, and already a hot flush flares over me.

"I'm going to mark you as mine, and when I wake you up in the morning, it will be with my tongue."

I half-huff and half-gasp, making a strange strangled sound as my knees weaken beneath me. He presses his body against mine, the thickness of his cock rock-hard against my stomach. My insides are melting, and I know this shifter will go to any length to win. But that is never going to happen.

Even if my body is begging me to kiss him first and then beg him to strip me with his mouth.

"A shame you won't win," I state.

"No?" His response taunts me.

The heat from his body is like an inferno, and his heavy breaths on my neck have me squeezing my thighs together. This man is a warrior, ripped and made for war, so I can only imagine how incredible it would be to have sex with him.

His fingers trail down my arms, and goose-bumps rise over my skin.

"Are you all right?" he whispers, while his thumb scrapes innocently over my stiff nipples.

It takes my breath away, and a shudder of pleasure drives straight to the apex between my thighs. Gods, I'm so wet. "You're not playing fair."

"This is how I kiss, cupcake." He leans his brow against mine. "I need to make sure you want this just as much as I do."

"Well, that's where you're mistaken. I feel nothing."

He throws his head back and roars with laughter. "Little woman, I can smell sweet slick filling the air. If I slid my hand to your tight pussy now, I would bring you to orgasm in seconds."

Swallowing hard, I try to hold myself together and not give in to him. "You make me so angry and horny at the same time, but that doesn't mean I can't resist."

"You want my touch, don't you? Clenching your thighs won't give you the release you crave."

His words send a shiver of excitement over me, and I want to wriggle so much and unleash the building pressure.

"You're struggling already," he tells me.

"Will you just kiss me and get this over with?" All I can think about is feeling him up against me. I'm high on the fumes of my own desire right now, and this Viking promises me things I desperately need. A rush of heat pours out of me.

His mouth clashes with mine suddenly. He kisses me harshly, violently, beautifully. His hands aren't on me, just his lips.

They kiss me with an unbearable passion, sucking on my lips, biting into the flesh, and there's something exhilarating to be with a man with such wildness.

I want to be lost to him, to have him carry me into this intoxication he promises.

When his tongue sweeps into my mouth, he explores me, and hell, his tongue is so long. I shake as he expertly draws mine into his mouth and sucks on it in a way that makes me think how glorious he will be going down on me. He seems like a biter, and shit, but I want his mark all over me.

With a grunt, he breaks away.

My lips feel swollen and sore in the most incredible way.

"Have you decided?" He growls, his eyes wild with lust.

I'm still battling the inferno of desire swallowing me while the ache between my thighs pulses. I'm so horny, I don't think I can stand it, and all he's done is kiss me.

"Maybe you need a bit more convincing," he says, his hand reaching for my pants, his fingers curling in over the band around my waist and pulling at it. "A bit of finger fucking?"

When I try to speak, my voice comes out all breathy, and I hate that all I can think about is needing release. The ache burrowing through is my wolf responding, calling to Bardhyl, needing him.

My pussy clenches at the thought of Bardhyl taking me.

"You lost for words, cherry pie?"

He pulls on my leggings, leaning in for another kiss. I hungrily cup his face and kiss him back this time. I can't even think straight, because the way he kisses is like being shot into the sky and floating on clouds. Like nothing can touch me. Like I am all he cares about. And I crave that feeling again and again.

His hand slides down the front of my pants until he finds the heat between my legs, the slick wetness that coats me.

My nipples tighten as he rolls a finger over my clit.

I kiss him harder, my world spinning with intensity. My hips rock back and forth as I clutch on to his shoulders. "Goddamn, Bardhyl," I murmur.

"What is it? You like the way my touch feels over your creamy pussy?"

"Stop talking, fuck!" I push down on his shoulders, needing him where I am about to explode.

But he fights me and looks me in the eyes. "Just so we're clear here, I've won, right?"

I pause for a second, my heart speeding, my desire crashing into me too fast. I can't even speak properly.

"N-No!" I shove against him, panting softly. But I'm fooling myself.

I've never seen a man stare at me like Bardhyl is now, promising me raw, primal sex. And shit, how the hell am I meant to come back down from this? "You play dirty."

His hand slips under my top, his palm so huge, I shiver with anticipation. "You're mine tonight, and you know it." He tugs on my top and rips it up and over my head, then tosses it somewhere behind him.

"You have perfect tits." His hands are on them, and I'm moaning, adoring the way he pinches my nipples to the point of pain, but I need more. "Say it," he says.

"What are you talking about?"

He pulls back his hands, and my skin quivers with the cold.

"That I won and you are mine for the night."

He grabs the top of my pants and yanks them

down my legs, leaving me naked. I gasp as he glances up from where he crouches in front of me.

"You haven't told me to stop yet."

But when his hand trails up my thigh and clasps my pussy, a whimper escapes my lips.

"That's what I thought."

Bardhyl

Her pussy is soaking wet, her slick driving me wild. She steps out of her pants, and I clasp on to her hips. Then I turn her away from me. She looks at me over her shoulder, her bronze eyes questioning me.

"Are you ready to say it?" I remind her, but when she doesn't respond, I run a hand up her back and force her to bend forward for me. She is spectacular, so stunning, and I now understand why Dušan and Lucien couldn't hold back.

"Place your hands on the wall."

She obliges, and I nudge open her legs with my foot, then I drop to my knees.

"Good girl. Now let me hear the words."

I take in all of her, her lips pink and swollen. Slick glistens on the inside of her thighs with her need.

Leaning forward, I take her scent inside me, my wolf shoving forward, well aware of what he needs to claim. I smell it too, a lot more than before… and I realize now that I have been wrong to think I had any resistance when it came to Meira.

My wolf snarls, bringing with it a sensation that rolls over my chest.

She's mine. She's my fucking mate, whether I wanted that or not. Our wolves are fated to be together.

Holy fuck! That complicates things, doesn't it?

"No more teasing," she moans. "You won. Are you happy? Now please, Bardhyl, fuck me."

I smile and love hearing her say those words. "Not quite yet, sweet cheeks."

"What more do you want? I'm giving you what you want. You can choke me, slap me, tug on my hair—anything."

Her eagerness sends pulses of arousal through me, and my cock punches hard to full erection. It hurts so much, and I'm dying to sink into her. But first I need to taste her. Grasping her ass, I pry apart her cheeks, seeing all of her. Then I press my mouth to her pussy, my face buried against her heat. She's like candy, sweet and musky and everything I could want

She moans instantly. I devour her, tugging on her folds, loving the sounds she makes, how she grinds herself against my face. My cock hardens, and I'm dying to fuck her. I eat her out savagely, her addictive screams turning me on even more.

I lick her from her little pussy all the way to her ass, taking all of her.

She trembles under me, and I feel she's close, but I'm not ready to have her go there. Not yet. So I pull away.

She groans in protest.

"Told you, gorgeous, that we do this my way." Up on my feet, I lift her with me, her back against my chest. My mouth is on her shoulder, licking her, taking mock bites. She has me wound us so tight that I'm barely holding on.

I carry her across the cave to the nest of leaves she built for us.

I twist her around in my arms and lay her down on her back. She stares up at me, her cheeks flush, and I see the hunger in her eyes. But there's something else. Her Omega side is controlling her.

Her breaths come heavy, and she clutches the ache in her stomach.

"Your body is craving an Alpha, and I'm going to be that for you, little Omega. It might even help your wolf."

"It won't make a difference. There's something wrong with me. This was a mistake." She moves away from me.

I lash out and take her arm, forcing her to face me. "Hey, enough. You're everything to me."

She scoffs. "Why? I told you before, I'm broken, and you shouldn't want me. I'm an idiot for letting myself get this far and believe that..." Her words trail off.

"Meira, I don't give a shit if you're from hell and sporting horns. I will dive into the darkness for you and with you."

She blinks at me, uncertainty flashing over her expression.

"Spread wide for me. I will show you."

I see the struggle behind her eyes where she wants to fight me, but she's way past the point of coming back. She's riled up, her wolf on the edge, and the pain she's feeling will worsen if she does nothing about her arousal. She obeys and her knees fall open. Light from the fire dances over her naked body. She's so beautiful.

Things are different now.

I should have sensed this before, but I refused to.

I'm not saying I have the answers, or even that I'm ready for dealing with a fated mate or Dušan's reaction.

But the answer stares me in the face. It curls around my heart like barbed wire.

Regardless of what tomorrow will bring, right now, it's all about Meira.

I get to my knees between her widening legs and lean forward as she watches me, worshipping my goddess. I take her heat into my mouth once again as she writhes, moaning louder, her hips rocking back and forth.

She tastes of euphoria, and I let myself fall.

I've been with enough women to know when someone special lands in my lap, and every lick, every inhale, every touch I make strengthens the bond between us. Energy lifts the hairs on my arms as it slides through my veins.

Her excitement escalates fast now, and I push a finger into her. She gasps, her chest arching, and fuck, I love the way her body reacts to me.

"You taste so damn good." I growl and kiss the inside of her thighs as I finger her faster. She's so juicy, and I add a second finger, squeezing it in there.

"Oh, Bardhyl." Her legs widen, and she shifts to fit me.

Meira's a delicious morsel, and I finger her quicker now, driving into her as she thrusts her pelvis with each push. Her cries grow louder, more intense. Fuck, she's gorgeous.

"God, you are so tight. When I stick my cock into you…"

She screams with her orgasm, and I bare my teeth then bite just above her small mound so she will always see my mark.

I taste her slick and blood, taking her into me, bonding us.

Her body convulses, her beautiful cries a song to my ears.

Before she finally quiets down, I pull my sticky fingers out and kneel in front of her. I wipe my mouth with the back of my hand, taking in her soaking cunt, the line of blood rolling from my bite, and this gorgeous naked woman spread out for me.

She draws in her lower lip between her teeth,

grinning at me so sexily. Gods, she wants this so badly.

I slide my hands under her ass and prop her up slightly for an easy angle to take her.

"You smell and taste so fucking incredible, cupcake. And I'm going to fuck that pretty, tight pussy," I rumble as I palm my cock and run the tip over her fire.

"I want you," she admits. "Please don't make me wait."

My heart hammers in my chest at her words, and I inch into her, slowly at first, until I get the right fit. Her walls squeeze around my dick, and I growl with desperation to drive into her.

She watches me, her hands clutching the blanket of leaves around her, her eyes dilated. She's as sexy as fuck. And she needs this.

I push into her all the way and fall forward, my hands on either side of her shoulders. She cries out, her body arching. Slowly at first, I draw out of her and go back in, then I pick up my pace to match her quickening moans. Her hands curl around my arms, holding on to me.

I fuck her harder, slamming into her. A blaze surges through me, and I roar as the intensity swallows me. She's so small, but she takes all of me, and her sweet groans wrap around me like a warm blanket.

She moans, curling her legs around my hips, while my gaze fixes on her bouncing breasts. Waves of bliss crash into me, sending shivers of power across my skin. My wolf shoves forward, calling to hers, craving her.

It doesn't take long for her to shudder, her head tilting back with the orgasm tearing through her. Just watching her, feeling her constrict me is the most magnificent feeling. And that's when I know I've come too far to back the hell away from her.

The tip of my cock swells inside her. I sense it pushing deeper and locking in place, knotting. Then it hits me, the climax racing through me like steaming water, my seed gushing out, ribbons of it filling Meira. I hiss, my body humming with ecstasy. It's how it works with Alphas and Omegas, how we ensure each fuck is a success to breed.

A howl bursts past my lips, my body shivering uncontrollably. White lights spark behind my eyes and I fill my little wolf.

When I finally float back down, I'm hunched over her, buried deep. It's where we'll stay until my swelling eases.

It takes us both a few minutes to ground

ourselves back to reality and readjust to our surroundings.

We're breathing fast, and her smile matches mine. I rub her nose with mine like Eskimos as I hold myself on all fours over the top of her, and she laughs. The sound is delicate and comes from in her gut.

"Fair to guess you don't have plans to fall asleep after this?" Her words are raspy, and her walls every so often clench around my cock, sending me into a frenzy of hisses as I lose the small amount of restraint I hold on to.

"You keep teasing me like that, squeezing me, and I'll keep you here for a week with me."

Her eyes widen. "I suspect Dušan wouldn't take too well to that."

I shrug. "He has to find us first." I'm talking out of my ass, but my head is still floating on the arousal, with lots of my blood filling my cock right now.

Meira clings to my arms, making no effort to pull back. Our faces are inches apart, her breasts squished to my chest.

"This is your fault, you know? Your stupid idea didn't go so well."

"From where I'm standing, it worked perfectly."

She sticks her tongue out at me, but her eyes are still glazed over from her orgasms. "Will you tell me about my blood test?" She whispers the question as though she's afraid I won't tell her.

"In the morning, I will. Not now." There is no way I can dump such news on her while I'm buried all the way inside her and we're locked together for a little while. I want her to focus on the joy she experienced, not what tomorrow will bring.

Waves of energy surge through my veins, the essence of my Alpha feeding her Omega the strength to eliminate the aches in her body. We're made for one another; it's as simple as that. No matter how pissed Dušan or Lucien may be, I can't change the nature of wolves and that we are fated mates as well.

After a long pause, she says, "You marked me, didn't you?"

"Of course. You're my fated mate, Meira. Have you not sensed this?"

Her grip tightens. "While we were having sex, I felt the connection like with Dušan and Lucien. But how can I have three mates?"

"It's common practice in Denmark. Women often take several husbands, and in some cases, men might take several females. But it all comes down to the selection of our wolves, and whom we were fated to mate with from our birth."

"That's pretty deep, to think our lives have been predestined for us."

I kiss her nose. "To me, it feels natural. We were meant to be together from the moment we took our first breaths. The hard part is finding each other."

She chews on her lower lip, a habit I notice of hers when she's worried about something, then she squeezes my cock as she shifts.

"Fuck, babe." I growl. "You keep doing that and I am never going to pull out."

"Oops." She smiles too beautifully to get mad at her.

I scoop an arm under her back and in one swift move, I roll onto my back, taking her with me, her legs still straddling me.

Now she's lying on top of me, me still embedded inside her gorgeous pussy.

She places her cheek to my chest, and I wrap her in my arms. I feel her thumping heart, hear the softness of her breaths. There's nowhere else I want to be. While we're locked together, she softens, and I like this side of her as well. We can't fight all the time.

"Tell me a story," she says.

I hold her tight and begin. "There was once a wolf, but she was so much more than she ever thought, for you see, she was half-beast, half-human."

She cranes her head up. "Is this a story about me?"

I hold back the laughter. "You'll find out if you keep quiet and listen."

She sticks her tongue out and squeezes her sweet pussy to prove her point. I hiss a breath, and if she keeps this up, I'm spanking her ass raw.

The woods around me bleed with shadows. Dušan trots alongside me, both of us in wolf form and carrying our clothes in our mouths. My jaw tightens, as I've been carrying my boots as well. They once belonged to my father, and there is no way I am leaving them behind. He had this obsession with the cowboy boots that he found on the side of the road. He took them, and they strangely fit perfectly. I lost him so long ago, and the boots are all I have left of him.

Morning brings blessed heat. The storms stopped just before dawn, but it was a wicked night of heavy rains pissing down and cracking thunder. Dušan and I had sheltered in an old abandoned shack, and in our wolf forms, we chased away the cold.

The rain washed away most scents, but when we discovered the fallen bridge, we knew we were definitely on the right path. There's a smaller rope bridge farther along the canyon's ridge that I discovered on my last visit to this area of the woods, which Bardhyl most likely wouldn't know about. That means they're still on the other side of the gorge. We move fast and cross over the narrow bridge made of rope and old wood panels.

Bardhyl would have shit his pants crossing this. Dušan takes rapid steps ahead of me, making the whole damn bridge wobble and shake.

Then we're running along the gorge, well aware Bardhyl would be headed in the direction of our home. My heart beats faster at the thought of seeing Meira again. I intend to keep her by my side every minute of the day until she accepts what she means to us and that being apart isn't going to work. She belongs to us and we to her. She just doesn't seem to realize that yet.

A twig snaps, and we freeze. I lift my nose and sniff the air, Dušan doing the same. Fresh rain. Muddy soil. And wolf. A she-wolf, more specifically, carrying a heavy air of slick. Meira. My heart gallops at the thought of finding her.

The cold wind blows directly in our faces, so she's ahead.

One look at Dušan, then we're off. We each spear outward to cover more ground.

The air thickens with her scent when I spot her racing alone through the woods at least fifteen feet away. My muscles ease at having found her, the tension rolling off me. Thank fuck! All I want now is to snatch her and kiss her until she sees sense.

She glances over her shoulder then keeps going. Has she ditched Bardhyl so easily? He's getting sloppy—or is something else chasing her? I wait a moment, studying the forest behind her, listening, but nothing comes.

She's running away. That's what she's good at, what she's always known, and it breaks me to see her doing it again after we offered her everything.

Fear strangles people, I get it, but she's our fated mate, and for that I will fight to the ends of the Earth to make her believe we won't let her walk away from us.

Not again.

Never again.

A growl rumbles through my chest as I watch

her running. On the other side of her, Dušan moves in her direction. That's my cue, and I dart toward our girl.

We travel like the wind.

Minimum sound.

Hunting what is ours. What belongs to us.

Dušan reaches her first, and she startles, a cry falling from her lips at seeing his wolf form. She backs away, hitting a tree, but she slips past it only to arrive face-to-face with me. I drop my clothes in front of me and call back my wolf.

"No!" she mutters as she looks over to Dušan standing before her as a man, naked.

"You are not supposed to be here," she continues, her voice quavering. Defeat finds her—it's written all over her face. And my heart aches to see her disappointment that we've found her. That's not the homecoming you want from your fated mate.

My body shakes, bones stretch, skin splits, and I bear the excruciating pain because it's gone as fast as it starts. Pain comes hand-in-hand with being a wolf, and I learned a long time ago that being afraid of it makes it worse. Now I embrace it. The more the change aches, the stronger it'll make me.

I rise to my feet in human form as Meira swings her attention my way, the tears in her eyes breaking me.

"This wasn't meant to happen," she murmurs. "Why can't you all see? I'm nothing."

With three long strides, Dušan reaches her, taking her arm. But she pushes him away.

I drag on my jeans, then pull on my long-sleeved tee and shrug into a jacket as I step into my boots. I stroll over as I straighten my shirt and jacket, my gaze again scanning the area for any sign of Bardhyl. Nothing. He's not around.

When Meira looks my way again, our gazes clash as mixed emotions crawl over her face. She's so scared that it's driving her decisions.

"You don't need to be afraid," I say as I stretch out an arm to her, but she just shakes her head.

"Don't. It drives me crazy standing here and not touching you. It wasn't this bad before." Her chin trembles as reality crashes into her thoughts. "If we just keep apart, our bond will break. It has to."

Her legs tremble, and Dušan scoops her up before she falls. He's still naked, which intensifies his connection with Meira, aiding her in healing quicker. The energy from my Alpha and me are overwhelming. Omegas *crave* Alphas. They need them for survival, and she's been away from us so long.

The ache she's experiencing is like someone has lit a match in her chest, causing the fire to spread wildly, burning her from the inside out. It comes from spending too much time away from the ones you're bound to. This is why we can't have her run away again, why she needs to fathom the danger.

"You're going to be all right now," Dušan coos, and she cradles against his chest. She looks so innocent and small. The opposite of her usual self.

I follow my Alpha out of the woods, grabbing his clothes off the ground in the process, and head into an area of land where the sun beams brightly. He drops to his knees and holds her against him. I kneel in front of him and reach over, pushing hair out of her face. Her scent hits me, heavy because she's so close. Sweet candy, just as I remember from when I went down on her, but there's something else. A masculine smell on her too. Bardhyl's.

He's claimed her. Fire slams into my chest to think he's laid with Meira. I've known him for years, know he wouldn't force himself on her... He wouldn't dare. What the fuck went down?

I meet Dušan's gaze, his eyes reflecting back my sentiment.

Bardhyl's smell is strong and reminds me of snow and dirt. Every wolf carries a unique signature, so there's no mistaking it was he who was with Meira.

Meira twists her head and looks at me, and I forget everything else. The primal instinct living inside me awakens, the savagery, the familiarity of what we have together. She feels it too, our connection like taffy pulled to the point of tearing.

"We missed you," I say, but she winces and pulls away, curling in on herself in Dušan's arms.

"Give her time," he says.

I dump Dušan's clothes near him and get to my feet as I stare into the surroundings, looking for any movements that would indicate undead are near. Time is what she needs for the pain of our reunion to settle down, for her to come to the realization that what we have is real and isn't going anywhere. I won't deny, though, that it stings like a bitch to have her pull away.

My thoughts slip back to my first fated mate, Cataline, taken by the undead. When she died, it felt like someone had scooped my heart right out of my chest while I watched. I never want to experience that again, yet here I am, connected to Meira, that same feeling crawling through me again.

"Go find him," Dušan orders, and I know exactly whom he's talking about.

I nod once and march back in the direction from which Meira came. I don't for a minute believe Bardhyl forced himself on Meira, but rather they had a similar connection as I have with her. Our wolves drew us together like magnets, the call impossible to resist.

We're animals programmed to breed. That's the core of what it comes down to. And sometimes, that connection is split. Bardhyl told me of women taking several men as mates in Denmark. Admittedly, it pains me to share Meira with two men, because I'm a greedy bastard—it makes me want to steal her away from everyone. Having her other mates being my best friends does ease the ache, though. I wouldn't accept them if they were strangers, or worse yet, someone I disliked. But I won't walk away if she takes Bardhyl into our relationship. I just need to make sure that is what happened between them.

I've been walking for over fifteen minutes, and my gut instinct tells me to return to Dušan. He's alone with Meira, and out here, we're the vulnerable ones.

A few more steps forward and a wall of stone peers back at me in the distance.

Caves.

I speed up and dart into the first one. It's empty, as are the next two, but in the fourth one, I hit the jackpot. The waft of a fire lingers in the air, as does the musky scent of sex. Twigs and a pair of boots litter the ground, and there are burned-out remnants of a small fire.

The sunlight behind me illuminates a figure rolling over onto his back, groaning like a bear.

Bardhyl squints in my direction. "Lucien?"

"Who'd you expect, Santa?" I tease, stepping deeper into the cave. He once told me he used to believe in the jolly bearded man, even when he was twelve.

Now that I'm closer, I can see his wrists and ankles are bound by vines. I chuckle while he growls at the realization that Meira attempted to tie him up. He rips the vines with sheer strength and his bare hands, then drags himself off the ground. He's naked, and his long blond hair resembles a bird's nest.

"Where is she?" he snarls, his shoulders squaring, his chest pumping rapidly with breath. His expression morphs into one of dread.

"Dušan has her. Get dressed, man. We need to go," I order.

His wide brow furrows, watching me. "She ran, then? Of course she did. That little minx is a fucking handful." He bends over and collects his jeans before climbing into them, followed by his shirt and boots.

"What the fuck happened in here last night?" I need to hear the truth from him.

He lifts his chin toward me. "Fuck, Lucien, she crawls under your skin. And being alone with her, it was impossible to resist the allure." He steps closer, rubbing his fingers through his hair. "It wasn't my intention to touch her. Her wolf called to mine like never before." He gives me a lopsided grin that makes him look stupid, but I know exactly what he's saying.

"You marked her?" My voice rises with a hint of jealousy.

"Yes," he admits immediately. Bardhyl has always been a straight shooter. Says it as it is. "As soon as I sensed she was my fated mate, I left my mark, hoping it would bring out her wolf. No fucking luck there."

"Shit. I've never faced someone with her condition before. What if her wolf is throwing off signals to all Alphas, and we're getting mixed signals too?"

Bardhyl snorts a laugh and claps me on the shoulder. "Have faith in the wolves, my friend. She may not be completely put together yet, but our wolves are smarter than you think. The mating game needs both sides to feel the eternal calling."

I shake him off and we march outside into the sunlight. I missed Meira like crazy, and now jealousy burns through me, but this is my darkness to deal with. If Meira's wolf selected Bardhyl as well as Dušan and me, then we're all in this together.

I shove him in the arm. "Fair warning. Dušan might be pissed. Your scent is all over her."

Bardhyl licks his dry lips and rolls his shoulders. "Won't be the first time he and I have clashed."

CHAPTER 12

MEIRA

I've never felt this level of intensity, and pain, and longing all at once. My body shudders, and the only relief comes from pressing as close as possible to Dušan. I can't even begin to make sense of how my wolf side works, but it's clear that I have zero control.

"You'll be okay," he reassures me as I loop my arms around his neck.

I breathe in his scent, and with each inhale, the aches dissolve. His presence is like oxygen to me. I take everything I need and he gives it to me, knowing exactly what will help.

Lifting my head, I stare into the bluest of eyes, brighter than the sky above us. His pitch-black hair flutters over his shoulders, and now I remember why I fell so easily for this Alpha. He's captivating and makes me forget that I am broken beyond repair. I mated with three Alphas who are my fated mates, who make me cry with desperation to be with them, and yet I've still failed them.

"You shouldn't have bothered," I whisper, my throat tightening.

"I had no choice, Meira. I need you like the air I breathe, and I would have gone insane if I never found you again. You know what I'm talking about, so how can you say that?"

A pulse dances in my neck, and I hate that my eyes prick. One moment, I finally escaped from Bardhyl. Next moment, I'm in Dušan's arms and drowning under his attention.

"I'm not enough for you, Dušan. Can't you see? Three Alphas marked me, but I'm still not good enough. It still wasn't enough for my wolf to come out." My voice trembles at how I don't feel complete. This is why it's easier to live alone. No one judges me, or reminds me of everything I'm not. "I want so much to hear you tell me you need me, that our life will be perfect, but I can't even promise you I'll be here tomorrow."

"Hush, don't say that shit," he coos. "Everything is fixable."

"You're not listening." I push my hands against his chest and wriggle out of his grasp. My feet are unstable at first, but I manage to stand on my own. "It kills me to leave you. My wolf is a stubborn bitch. She won't come out, yet she makes me suffer, longing for you, insisting I need to be with you. But then what?"

He reaches an arm out to me as he stands, looming over me. But I push his hand away.

"How's it going to work, Dušan?" I grip my hips. "We pretend all is good, then one night when we all sleep happily my wolf decides to tear out of me, killing me, and then slaughtering my Alphas? And if not that, wolves will start a war when they find out I'm immune to the undead and see me as some kind of cure." I wipe away the tears leaking out of the corner of my eyes. "Why do you want to live with a ticking time bomb?"

He snatches my arm and forces me against him. I stumble forward, our bodies colliding. "If I'm going to die, I couldn't think of a better way than at your wolf's teeth."

I frown at him. "Don't mock me."

His hand around my back strengthens. "I mean every word, Meira. But that's not going to happen. We need to keep trying to help you. Now that we know why you're sick, it might be the key to unlocking this situation with your wolf."

Bardhyl's words about the blood test come to mind. "What did my bloodwork show?"

But instead of responding, he twists his head to look over his shoulder as Lucien and Bardhyl stroll toward us. I push myself out of Dušan's arms, torn in too many directions, my emotions a tangled mess.

Stay.

Buy myself time.

Escape from these three is impossible. So that option is gone.

What I need is to understand what Dušan discovered in my blood. Maybe there is a chance to make this work and heal me by some miracle.

The air suddenly grows thick as Dušan turns to Bardhyl with a sense of hostility I don't expect.

"With me!" Dušan barks at Bardhyl, who glances my way and winks before walking off with his Alpha.

"What's going on?" I mutter toward Lucien, who doesn't pay them attention but only has eyes for me.

"Are you hurt?" he asks.

I shake my head. "Tell me what's going on with

them." I don't mean to snap, but I don't want Bardhyl hurt because of what we did last night. What happened was mutual on both sides. And if he's one of my fated mates, then Dušan and Lucien need to accept that.

"Dušan is Bardhyl's True Alpha, and that means answering to him."

I jerk my head up. "Answering to him about being with me last night?"

He nods. "About marking what's his."

Fire fuels my words. "From what I understand, you three are mine as much as I am yours, so we should have a say in this together."

Lucien smirks. "You've been listening to Bardhyl too much. What the Denmark pack does and what Ash Wolves do are not always aligned. But they will sort it out, even if it comes down to a fight."

I stiffen. "What the hell? Did you fight Dušan too? That's barbaric!"

As though he can't stand it a second longer, he reaches over and takes my arms, drawing me against him. "We are barbarians, my little bird, and our Alpha Dušan has the right to accept or reject another man for his fated mate."

"But it's my wolf who picks!"

"And Dušan gets the final say, even if it breaks your heart and Bardhyl's. What Dušan says is law. You will have Dušan and me, so your Omega wolf won't suffer."

I hate the sound of this. Fury churns in my chest because what I felt with Bardhyl is animal-istic and wild and... well... I don't know what to make of my feelings, but I should get to make that choice, not Dušan.

I spin on my heels and march in the direction of the woods where Dušan and Bardhyl vanished when strong arms clasp around my waist and whip me up off my feet.

"I can't let you do that," Lucien whispers.

"Why the hell not?"

"Trust me. Men just need to get shit off their chests sometimes, and both Alphas have dark pasts they may not be ready to share with you."

That statement leaves me stunned, and suddenly I feel like I don't know any of these men.

I shove myself out of Lucien's grasp. How in the world can I be so needy for their attention, have their presence physically eliminate the pain their absence caused, and yet have them seem like strangers on another level?

"What's *your* dark secret then?" I blurt out,

eyeing him up and down. "Is it related to your cowboy boots?"

His face loses some of its color at my question, and it's clear I've taken him off guard. He never blinks his steel-gray eyes, while the breeze ruffles his short, brown hair. He's six-foot-three, rugged and smoldering, everything about him screaming *wolf*. My attraction to him started the second we met by the side of the road when he picked up Dušan and me. Even now, standing before him, all I can think about is going to him, tasting his lips, remembering how he claimed me. But I stand my ground, wanting answers. Lucien is everything I've ever desired in a man, and he looks at me with hunger.

But he doesn't make a move, either.

"The boots are all I have left of my father," he finally answers. "And if you need to know the truth, I lost my first fated mate not that long ago to the undead. So yeah, we all have dark shit in our past, Meira. And we deal with it the only way we know how. It's why you run, isn't it? It's all you've ever known."

I can't move or even find my voice, as what he's said weighs heavily on my mind. There are so many questions I contemplate asking, yet only one pushes forward. "Y-You already found your fated mate?"

He runs a hand through his hair and glances to his feet momentarily before meeting my gaze. "Until I met you, I still dreamt of her. They say a true fated mate is for life, but that isn't the case. Look at us. We all come from twisted pasts, and we are bound to you." He stands tall, and his stormy irises lock on to mine, making it clear he whole-heartedly believes every word he says. But part of me worries that maybe I can't live up to his initial mate. He loved her first, and she will always be with him. What if I'm not good enough?

I want to apologize for my earlier anger at him, to draw him in my arms, because I struggled severely from being away from the Alphas over a few days, and it would have been a lot worse without Bardhyl next to me. I can't even imagine how losing her felt. But the thought of losing one's mate brings back the heartache from when my mama died. It was so long ago, yet it feels like it happened yesterday, and that familiar sharpness in my chest rises again.

Striding closer to him, I slide my hands in his, our fingers interlacing, and I just hold him, because no words can ease the grief.

Three Alphas, each so similar but so different.

Dušan is the one in charge, dominating and never letting his guard down.

Lucien brings patience and understanding to our group, but there's a fire in his eyes that makes him unpredictable.

Bardhyl's the joker, but he's using that to hide the real him. It's so obvious.

And me… I complete the circle of misfits by being shattered and lost.

Maybe I'm where I should be, among these three. After all, we're all trying to find out where we belong in this world, right?

An ear-piercing howl slices through the silence, and I flinch, my head jerking in the direction of the woods Dušan and Bardhyl disappeared in.

Dread flares over me, and I jump into a run toward them.

"Meira," Lucien yells, his footfalls hitting the ground right behind me. He snatches my arm and swings me back around, but my fury lashes out.

I slam my palms against his chest and catch him off guard, judging by his widening eyes, but he doesn't let go of me. My breaths are coming out as pants, and all I can think is that Dušan is beating up Bardhyl, deciding *for* me who I can or can't be with. Pent-up tension has me thrashing to free myself.

"Let go! He's going to hurt Bardhyl."

Lucien breaks out into a laugh at my expense.

"Meira, it'd take an army to physically hurt Bardhyl. That's the first thing you need to know about your Viking warrior. Now come here." He wrangles me roughly and spins me around so his chest is flush against my back, his arms clasped around the front of my shoulders, keeping me in place.

"Then why can't I go—"

Two wolves burst out from the woods with such ferociousness, I flinch against Lucien, losing my words. One as black as night, Dušan, the other with the whitest fur and black-tipped ears. Bardhyl. Together, they're a jumbled ball of teeth and growls, the battle savage.

My heart hammers and I go rigid, but I'm not backing away. Lucien's lips are on my ear. "The thing about Ash Wolves is that most things between Alphas are resolved through battle."

I shudder and clench my teeth. "Why the hell isn't Dušan accepting Bardhyl? It's my call!" Writhing against Lucien does nothing to free myself.

"Quite the opposite," he murmurs, his chin resting on my shoulder. "Watch them fight. It's all mock. There's no blood. This is a fight of power and aggression and reconfirming hierarchy. Bardhyl took something that belonged to the Alpha, and now Dušan must reestablish his position before he accepts the Viking being with you. Bardhyl has to kneel."

The more I watch, the more I start to notice he's right. The pair roll on the ground in a tangle, biting at each other's necks and sides and hides, ripping fur but not drawing blood.

Looking at it through different lenses now, there's an aggressive beauty about the fight.

I don't understand most of these pack rules or the power struggle, but I'm slowly learning new things every day. Things I missed out on while growing up mostly with other females and then on my own.

Dušan latches on to the back of Bardhyl's neck and tosses him across the ground with ridiculous strength. Bardhyl slides into a tree and stays down as his Alpha trots over to him and sniffs him.

"See here," Lucien says. "He'd normally unleash a howl of victory, but that's not going to work in our favor out here."

I swallow hard as Bardhyl climbs up, head low, and darts past his Alpha to vanish into the shadowy woods. Moments later, Dušan comes toward us. His body shakes as he pulls himself up into a human, transforming so fast that by the third step, he's completely taken human form. Fur has vanished, his face morphed back to his gorgeous self.

Bite marks and bruises mar his body, but it doesn't distract from how powerful and utterly naked he is. My gaze falls to the thatch of dark hair above his cock, flaccid but still big… and of course, I lack any ability to act discreetly.

He catches me staring, and my cheeks flush with fire.

I shift to move out of Lucien's arms, but he holds me still as Dušan approaches. Strong and powerful, he stops inches from me and grabs my chin, forcing me to face him. A fresh scratch under his eye blushes red. He only has eyes for me.

I'm pinned between these two Alphas, and I need to ask what the resolution was with Bardhyl and if he's coming back, but instead I'm lost under Dušan's wild, hypnotic stare. My body hums with energy, their energy blending in with mine.

"You've selected three of us as your mates, and I accept that. But no more, understand?" he growls.

"It's not like I consciously wanted three," I respond, my muscles tensing. I don't know if it is or isn't, but my wolf seems to be in heat around these three Alphas.

"Maybe not, but I won't tolerate another."

Bardhyl returns toward us, already dressed. His head is low, and I find it fascinating how loyal and dedicated wolves are to their Alpha.

Dušan lets out a deep, throaty growl, filled with dominance, sexual desire, and a reminder of all of our positions in his pack. I feel the vibrations of his power like never before, and my breath catches in my throat.

He nods to Lucien, who releases me, and it's Dušan who takes hold of me now, by my neck, and draws me to him. Our lips clash with a savage hunger. And just like he put Bardhyl back in his place, I know exactly what's coming my way.

His canine nicks my lip, and he licks my blood, the pinch stinging. His hands tighten on my hips. I can barely breathe from the heat he pours over me.

"You are mine." He snarls in my mouth and pulls back, his eyes taking wolf form.

Instinct has me wanting to kiss him back

harder, but I stand my place in front of him. My wolf picked him and the others, so that means finding a way to make this work.

"We should leave," Lucien says, interrupting the buildup. The way Dušan's hand has grabbed at my top, it's like he might rip it off me here and now.

"Time isn't on our side with her sickness," Lucien continues.

Sickness? My blood runs cold. I turn around, surrounded by my three shifters, and look at each of them. "What did my blood test show?" I ask, meeting each of their stares.

"She doesn't know yet?" Dušan asks Bardhyl.

"Nope," Bardhyl answers, his voice hard.

"Is this the place to do it?" Lucien questions.

"Hell yes," I say, butting in. "I'm not moving from this spot until you tell me."

Maybe I'm a comedian, because all three of them laugh at me, but I don't appreciate being mocked for standing up for myself to three powerful men.

I dig my heels in. "I'm not kidding around," I snap. "Someone tell me what the fuck is going on with me."

They exchange looks, and it's Dušan who cups my face and leans in. "Meira," he starts off tenderly, and already I can tell he's going to say something bad.

"Just say it. Don't sugarcoat it, please." My stomach coils in on itself. The longer they take to tell me, the worse the scenarios my mind comes up with are.

He kisses me on the mouth, then pulls back with a look of regret washing over his face. "Meira, baby girl, you have leukemia."

"Oh, Meira," Dušan murmurs, his hands sliding over my shoulders. His attempt to smile comes out crooked and holds a sense of guilt, as if the news was somehow his fault. "This is why we had to find you so quickly. The disease is slowly working through your human body, and your wolf is the only way you'll survive."

I read about human illnesses when I once broke into an old library for shelter. The building had been ransacked, but some books still remained. From what I recall, it's a blood disorder, a cancer of blood cells. It stops the body from fighting bacteria and viruses, and… I know there was other stuff in the book, but I can't remember the rest.

"Meira," Dušan says softly.

But as the information sinks through me, the tears fall. I must have done something awful in my previous life to have so much bad luck in this one.

I sob into my hands, and Dušan gathers me into his arms, his chin over my head, his hand rubbing my back. Here he is, still naked like it's natural, and I'm falling apart. Everything feels surreal. He kisses my brow and my fingers. But all I can think about is if my wolf had just come out, it'd have solved everything.

"Leukemia is what's been making you immune to the undead, and your wolf side has kept you alive this far."

I raise my chin and lower my hands while he wipes my tears with his thumbs.

"Your results showed that your human body is starting to break down and..." He licks his lips, seeming to struggle to find his words.

"What is it?" I ask, needing to know exactly what's going on with me.

Lucien and Bardhyl approach us, one standing on each side of me.

Dušan says in a whisper, "It's progressing quickly. Within maybe a week or two, it will spread to your organs. It's why you've been vomiting blood, why we need to find a way to bring out your wolf."

Dread throbs under my skin. It's one thing to hear I have a disease that might be stopping my wolf from coming out, but now I'm being told I only have two weeks left to live at most. I can't fathom the news. Here I worried that staying with the Alphas put them in harm's way, while a bigger danger lurked over me.

I can't breathe. My knees weaken, threatening to collapse.

As if my illness wants to remind me this is shit is real, a tremendous ache spreads through my whole body, ripping at me as if someone has whipped me.

My legs give out and I cry, hugging my middle. I wrench over, and the pain spews out past my throat, coating the grass with blood. I feel better getting it out of my system, but it doesn't remove the reality of my shitty situation.

Lucien is at my side, pulling my hair over my shoulders.

Everything is too unbearable now. Numbness crawls through my limbs, and I look from one Alpha to another, each offering me hope. But I sense their fear, too, that it may be too late. How could things have gotten so bad?

I've been different my whole life, and I never let it stop me.

When I look up and wipe my mouth with my sleeve, I blink at my three men.

Powerful Alphas here to help me.

They owe me nothing, but they don't turn away. The burning in my chest lingers, but it's less painful now.

Every second ticks away in my mind.

Bardhyl offers me a reassuring smile, and Lucien takes off his jacket and hands it to me to wear while Dušan dresses himself. Then he stretches out a hand to me.

"Let's go home."

I doubt anything will be the same again. How can it be? I tried to go back to the way things were, believing I was doing the right thing. But I was wrong.

So now, I'll take these wolves' guidance and try it their way. I slide my arms into Lucien's black leather jacket. It floods me with warmth, his wolf scent like a reassuring blanket cocooning me. It falls to my thighs and keeps the cold at bay. Then I place my hand in Dušan's.

"I'm ready," I admit. Ready to survive. After all, there are two options in front of me, right? The one where I continue following Mama's instructions to keep running, to not trust anyone, to use what I have to continue living. Then there is the one where I place my trust in these stubborn, dominating Alphas who won't give up on me. Who promise me a new world.

Me.

Meira.

The lonely girl who lived on the fringe of the world.

Who's now desperate to find a way to survive in Shadowlands while everything else tries to kill me at every turn.

I squeeze Dušan's hand so he knows I'm set on following him. This is my last chance, so I take it.

He offers me a smile that warms my heart and sinks down into my soul.

"First thing I'm doing is eating half a goddamn boar," Lucien states.

Bardhyl chuckles. "Only half? You've grown soft."

There's comfort in their banter, like somehow I belong here, though at the back of my mind, I have mixed emotions. I barely know these Alphas, even after everything we've been through. This is new, and giving in has never been something I do.

But going with them… It doesn't feel like *giving in* right now. It feels like hope.

Dušan

Fuck.

The word just keeps sliding over my thoughts. It never occurred to me once that Meira might gain yet another fated mate. I'd seen no signs of it back at the compound.

Fated mates are for life.

This bond is not just between Meira and me, but with Lucien and Bardhyl as well.

I don't cross swords, and I'm sure they don't, either, but that's not even what bothers me. It's not having Meira all to myself all the time that I need her.

What the hell am I meant to do? These men are my closest friends, and I won't lose them or have Meira hate me for denying her the ability to be with them.

Yeah, the situation is bullshit, and fuck yeah, I'm jealous. But like most things in my life that don't go to plan, which is a fucking lot, I improvise.

We've been walking for a few hours now, and I can't stop staring at Meira, even if I try. She's constantly on my mind. And it bothers me a hell of a lot that I don't know how we're going to work out our situation. Allocated visits? Fuck that. The decision will come to me once we get home, so I shove those thoughts aside for now.

Priority is getting home in one piece and finding a way to save her. And until then, I sure as fuck don't want her thinking I'm an asshole. I swallow my jealousy and distract myself by surveying the woods we pass through, listening to sounds, anything that will give us an edge to get the hell out of here fast.

I crave her, and the savage urge to drag her into my arms and claim her right now up against a tree grows by the second. The urge to strip her and fuck her so she remembers her Alpha grows through me.

Timing sucks.

Location sucks.

Fuck, I just need a damn break, a minute for things to stop sucking.

Lucien walks ahead of us, Bardhyl at our backs, and we travel silently.

Her eyes flicker in my direction, then look away quickly when I catch her staring. What is she thinking? That I'm a monster?

We live in a world full of dark creatures, and in order to survive, you must become one. She'll either accept that or she'll struggle to find happiness.

For fuck's sake. I have to get my head straight and stop whining.

We're downwind, and the next rush of air brings with it a new smell… wet dog fur, muskiness, perspiration.

Wolves.

My hands fist into balls, and fury rises along with my wolf within me. The presence of any uninvited wolves on our land is a hostile sign and a declaration of war against us.

We all cease our marching in unison. Lucien's head lifts as he takes a deep breath. "At least five or six of them. A small pack."

I clasp Meira's hand and draw her to me.

"Rogue wolves?" she murmurs.

"Those bastards rarely work together, and if

they do, never in these numbers." I glance over my shoulder to Bardhyl. "Scout out the pack," I order.

He lifts his chin, his jawline clenching. "Think it's in any way related to Mad?"

"Doubt it, but I won't discount anything right now. They wouldn't have picked up our scent yet, so we have the element of surprise on our side."

One nod and he sidesteps past us, then darts into the woods without a sound.

Dread lifts the hairs on my nape. Not for me, but for Meira. We don't have time for this shit, and I don't want her harmed.

"Anywhere we go, they'll track her scent down," Lucien says.

"Then we fight and rip their fucking heads off." I suck in rapid breaths, and my wolf bristles at the mention of a battle. "And one eye on Meira at all times."

"If we could track down some undead, maybe I could hide among them if we tie them up?" she suggests.

"Love the idea, but we haven't encountered any. We stay low until Bardhyl returns."

Lucien charges ahead of us, searching for a safe spot. We know the drill, have done this too many times when we hunted for Omegas. We've been ambushed before by rogue wolves, but we've never had a pack on our land.

My muscles knot up, and a pang of fury has me riled up.

"I need a weapon," Meira states. I draw a blade from the back of my belt and hand it to her, hilt first.

"Don't hesitate to use it. Don't give the enemy a chance. You see an opportunity, strike." I push a hand through her hair and draw her closer to me. "Nothing will happen to you, I give you my word."

"Does she have a name?" she asks, lifting my blade.

I want to laugh at her cuteness. "No, but I've always seen it as a male over a female."

She studies the leather hilt, running her thumb over it. "Feels feminine to me."

I eye her, not sure if she's insulting me or the army knife that is thick and razored on one end, but I let it go. "You can call it what you want, babe, as long as you use it when needed."

Taking her elbow, I guide her to a shadowy part of the woods, where dampness fills the air and will mask our scent easier.

Lucien returns to us in moments, wild-eyed and nodding. "There's an old rundown farmer's cottage down the hill close to the water. But we'd be spotted going down there, so it's not an option for now."

"Then we stay low and wait," I say.

Meira tucks my knife into her boot, and we sink down to our knees near several oversized shrubs. They'll conceal us in case someone moves fast past the area. The problem is more to do with the smell my little Omega emits, calling to others like a dinner bell.

First, work out what the hell we're dealing with, then we finish this. We're too far from our compound, but I have two of my strongest warriors with me. I could do with a good fight right now.

Meira bites down on her lower lip, staring out into the woods around us. "If we can bypass them, maybe that's for the best," she suggests.

Except that's not the world I live in. Running away isn't an option. Intruders are in my backyard, and no one else will drive them away before they cause damage. My pulse is thumping, my heart pounding with adrenaline at what's coming our way, and I can't fucking wait.

"We never run from the enemy," Lucien whispers to Meira. "We always fight."

"When we go back, I want someone to teach me how to fight properly and use weapons," she says, and hell, I might just love her for that.

I lean over and kiss her cheek, then sweep over to her lips. "You got it."

A leaf crunching draws my attention behind me, and I jerk my head up, my hands fisted, ready to lunge, Lucien doing the same.

Bardhyl bursts out of the shadows, and I stand to meet him as he speaks. "Seven males. Two are Alphas, others are Betas. And they're coming this way."

"Good. We spread out and wait, then we jump. Go for the Alphas first." I flick my hands at my men to show them the best spots to wait before we attack.

The wind direction is in our favor, and I want this over with fast.

I crouch back down next to Meira. "Stay here. I'll be close. Anyone comes near you, you scream."

She nods quickly and her cheeks pale. I don't blame her for being afraid. I'm so damn tired of these complications preventing us from getting home.

I kiss her on the brow and jolt to my feet, ready, leaving her kneeled down.

It's barely a split second that passes when a guttural growl erupts from behind me.

Blood drains from my face, and I whip around to find a huge timber wolf shifter standing over my startled Meira, his teeth bare as a growl rolls through his chest, ears pressed flat to his head. Sonofabitch… He has every intention of taking Meira.

CHAPTER 14

MEIRA

$\mathcal{I}$ dig my fingers into the soft soil as my heart hits the back of my throat. Coldness sweeps through me, bringing with it the reality of how much shit I'm in.

I flinch and look over my shoulder as a gray wolf stands inches behind me. Hot breath washes over my back, his growl reverberating so loudly, it seeps into me. I can't stop shaking. My gaze swings back to Dušan, who stands six feet away, blood draining from his face. Bardhyl is close by, and Lucien is nowhere in sight.

Dušan straightens, his shoulders broad, his demeanor transforming into a powerful Alpha before my eyes. Anger now lashes his features, his upper lip twisted.

"Why are you on my land?" Dušan barks loudly, nostrils flaring, voice flooded with menace. Shadows gather under his eyes, and there's no way in hell I want to ever cross him when he looks this furious. But right now I welcome it, want him to tear apart the creature looming over me.

"You get one chance," Dušan warns. The air thickens with the scent of his wolf and the energy of an oncoming transformation. His eyes have already morphed into his wolf's.

My skin is littered with goosebumps from the war I'm in the middle of.

Fear swells inside my mind, slipping into my veins, except I'm not alone anymore. I have three Alphas who will fight for me… *with* me.

I feel the weight of the knife in my boot, but I don't reach for it, not yet. I stay kneeling on the ground, waiting for the right moment. I have no damn idea when that is, though.

No one dares move an inch.

Shadows slink around the woods surrounding us, circling us, cornering us. More wolves.

I want to warn my men, but I am under no illusion my Alphas aren't already aware of the additional intruders.

My heart speeds.

Then in a crazy moment of silence, everything changes.

Thundering steps strike the earth at my right. I turn just as Lucien, still in his human form, lunges at the wolf behind me.

Lucien slams into him, dragging him away, but not before the enemy bites into my shoulder.

Sharp pain slices into my flesh, and my screams bleed into the air as I'm dragged down from the momentum.

I'm drowning in agony while commotion explodes around me. I hit the ground with a loud smack, and I swear I'm going to scream from the exhaustion of constantly getting hurt and being in danger.

For those few seconds, I feel nothing but the racing adrenaline taking me over.

I rush to my feet, my hand going to my boot. Knife in hand, I stagger backward, shudders tearing through me.

Lucien strangles the wolf with his bare hands as the creature jerks to his feet, and I can't breathe from the terror colliding into me.

Sounds of battle burst from my other side. I whip around as Dušan battles two wolves. Bardhyl, in his white wolf form, roars with fury as another two wolves collide with him.

I should go help, but I can't even stand upright steadily.

When a shadow emerges from my right, I turn in its direction. A brown wolf with white-tipped ears and dark eyes prowls toward me. I lift my weapon because I'm not fast enough to outrun him.

I know better than to run, anyway. It would only further spark the wolf's desire to show his dominance over me. Doesn't stop my legs from shaking.

"Don't come any closer," I threaten, my fingers tightening around the knife's hilt until my knuckles turn white.

This is my fight as much as the Alphas'. I edge past a pine tree, my eyes never leaving the enemy.

Head low, he slinks closer, a deep, guttural sound rolling from his chest. I twist away, the air rushing out of me as an overbearing fear squeezes my chest.

Then he charges.

An involuntary scream spills past my throat as I swipe my blade, the sharp edge catching the animal on the side of his nose.

He growls and bowls into me, knocking me over. In seconds, Lucien wrenches the wolf off me just as fast.

I scramble backward on my ass over the forest floor, gasping for air.

Lucien lifts the wolf and tosses him away from me. How the hell does he have such strength?

He's at my side, blood smeared across the cuts on his neck and arm. He smiles like somehow everything will be all right. In that very moment, a burning ache from the bite on my shoulder sinks through me, like someone has poured boiling water over my skin. I wince at the blood staining my top.

"Stay close to me." Lucien heaves each breath. He grabs me, his fingers tightening on my wrist as he hauls me alongside him.

Dušan howls victoriously with two wolves slain at his feet, then leaps to Bardhyl's aid, as the white wolf has four attackers surrounding him. Lucien doesn't go to his aid but holds me close while my head whirls with fear that we'll be captured.

That's when a shrill whistle pierces through the woods.

We freeze, listening for more sounds.

A figure strolls out of the shadows, a shifter in

human form, dressed in jeans and a gray hoodie. The stranger is tall and may not be as broad as my men, but there is an energy around him. More wolves in animal form join him. The shuffling sound behind me draws my attention to the small pack pulling away from Bardhyl and Dušan to join their Alpha.

Only when this stranger fully emerges from the darkness do I see him clearly. He's not old—maybe in his early thirties—brown hair parted on the side messily and hanging over one eye. His chin is wonky, like it's healed from a bad accident. And he looks familiar… like we've encountered each other before. I wrack my mind, but I've crossed paths with so many people, most for short periods of time. They flash in my thoughts, except most memories I pushed away long ago. Most fall into one of two categories. Those who've hurt me, or those who died and left me messed up. Which means whoever this guy is, well… he's got to be an asshole.

"Meira," he says, sending my stomach plunging to my feet because he remembers my name when I can't recall his face. "I've been searching for you. Heard from a little girl who spoke of a Meira in these woods, so we came to investigate."

"You better not have hurt her," I snap, my weapon raising. I'll gut the weasel if he did something to Jae.

"You actually care? Since when?"

At hearing the slight lisp he has, I start to remember. Not long after Mama died, I met him during one of my stays in a town in northern Transylvania, where small fractions of packs appear all the time. It's a wild area where fights for small pockets of land just outside Dušan's territory occur daily. I met this man in a small community area. I was younger, lost in the world, and I trusted him when he offered me shelter and food.

But in exchange, he wanted what I wouldn't give. That night he called me his Omega and tried to rape me, so I kicked him in the balls. The bastard beat me up until my eyes were so swollen, I couldn't see a thing. All those memories, the ugliness of the world, my fear, blended into a mess I tucked in the farthest recesses of my mind. I had intended to forget them… and I sure as hell don't want to bring those memories back now.

That's the reason I ended up living alone, why I made a treehouse, why I never helped anyone else. It's been so long, but now seeing him again, I'm trembling.

"You owe me," he snarls. "And I'm here to collect."

"What the hell is he talking about?" Lucien snaps, holding me closer to him. Dušan in human form, Bardhyl as his wolf, join us, confronting the intruders. Four of us against maybe fifteen of them. Are there more wolves out there, watching us from the shadows? How long have they been tracking us if Bardhyl only spotted a handful earlier?

I spit on the dirt and offer him a sneer. It's more than Evan deserves. "You're a bastard. You beat me up and tied me to a fucking tree, then left me for days."

Dušan stiffens beside me and steps forward. "She owes you nothing. But you are trespassing on my land. I'm the Alpha of Shadowlands Sector, and you will pay with blood."

Evan scoffs as if the threat means nothing to him. "I protected her from the men who planned to steal and rape her between them. And she screamed bloody murder when I touched her. Frigid bitch." He looks over to me, flicking his head in an attempt to shift the lock of hair out of his eyes, but it never moves. "I tied you up as a lesson. But you escaped, didn't you? You know how much I had to pay those men in resources to leave you alone, to not go after you? You should be thanking me." He sets a splayed hand to his chest like somehow his words are heartfelt. "Now, I come for my payment, which I'll take in the form of rutting you over and over."

Bardhyl unleashes a snarl that comes so sudden and loud, it makes me jump in my skin.

"I don't have fucking time for this bullshit," Dušan growls. "Leave, or you end up like them." He points his chin to the dead wolves at my left. "That's my only peace offering."

No one responds, and Evan rolls his eyes, slouching on one leg, eyeing his large group and then the four of us. Yeah, that part worries me too. But I'll die before I let this asshole claim me. Looks like I'm fighting.

Lucien's hand is on my waist, and he has me glued to his side. He looks down at me for a smidgen, whispering while Evan talks shit to my Alphas. "In a second, all hell will break loose. Get up a tree as fast as you can. It'll be easier for you to defend yourself, as you can fight them back with a branch to keep them from climbing after you. Understand? I'll try to stay near."

Before I can even respond, energy collides into

me from my Alphas transforming. The air ripples with their musky, powdery scents.

"Your time's up," Dušan declares. He shifts into his wolf form and jumps into attack, Bardhyl and Lucien on his heels.

I dart backward. Running, I scan for the best tree and spot one with lower branches and thicker clusters of leaves for concealment.

But before I can reach my haven, someone slams into my back, throwing me forward onto my face.

My cries are muffled by the mouthful of dirt I just ate. I whip around the moment weight lifts off my back and swing my blade, catching the unsuspecting bearded man across the gut. It's not deep, but it's enough to draw blood and distract him.

I kick him hard in the shin, and as he bowls over, I run to get out of there. Choosing a different tree to simply escape this asshole, I skid around the battle and finally climb up a perfect one with enormous high branches and lots of foliage.

My hands grasp the lower branch as my legs quickly swing up and around, when a sudden sharpness bites into my ankle and tugs down on me. But I hold on desperately and kick wildly. I look down to the gray wolf latched on to my leg, and another coming closer. I kick him aggressively in the nose, and with a whimper, he releases me.

Hastily, I scamper up the tree, shoving past the prickly branches ladened heavily with round, deep green leaves. The bark on this trunk scratches the hell out of my skin.

From up here, I scan the area.

The wolves battle. Teeth and fur and growls.

The aggressive sounds they emit leave my skin crawling. I don't know if I can ever fight that way.

A growl sounds below me. I look down, and the damn bearded man is back, his eyes as gray as his stormy skin, his upper lip sitting at an odd angle from an old injury. I shake with anger.

I tuck my knife into my boot and reach up to grab a thinner branch with spiky offshoots. With both hands, I yank down on it, the wood cracking and snapping free. Lurching backward from the motion, I fling out a hand and snatch the trunk to steady myself.

"No use hiding, bitch," he snarls.

I sidestep to stand on a branch directly above him. He's not so skilled at getting up here, luckily. So I haul the branch, shoving a shoulder against the tree for balance. My feet spread over a platform of crisscrossing branches, and I spear my weapon downward.

It jams right into his head and scrapes down the side of his face. He cries out from the shock, his hands cartwheeling as he falls and hits the ground hard. His face is bloody, and *ouch*, I did a lot more damage than I thought. Fuck, yeah.

Lucien was onto something in telling me to hide up here.

The torturous sounds from the battle have me twisting around toward other wolves who are rushing my way. I clutch onto my branch, my insides wound so tightly, I might be sick.

They snarl at the base of the tree while the bearded man gets up. I shove the weapon at him, but the dick grabs it and wrenches it away with unimaginable strength, taking me with it as I lose my footing.

My death flashes before my eyes as the ground flies up toward me. A shrub breaks my fall, poking and stabbing me. I groan, as every inch of me feels like it's on fire. I keep expecting teeth to tear into me and rip me apart.

Strong hands grab my ankles, and I'm wrenched across the ground. I cry out and reach for anything to use as a weapon. Fistfuls of dried leaves aren't going to help me.

I spin on my side, thrashing against the bearded asshole who's smirking at me with blood-stained teeth from where I'd hurt him. He deserves a hundred times worse.

"Let me go." I toss everything I can grab at him and attempt to push myself up to reach my boot for my blade, but it's impossible. He yanks me so fast, I have leaves and twigs rushing up on the inside of my top.

I keep thrashing and wriggling against him, screaming out while two of the enemy wolves follow close behind. When he finally drops my legs, I can't see my Alphas or the battle.

I reach for the knife in my boot as wolves snarl in my ear and the guy in front of me unbuckles his belt.

"I smell your slick," he mutters, and suddenly, I'm going to be sick.

Darkness spirals around me, and bile hits the back of my throat. My fingers grasp the knife.

I'm shaking horrendously, because if we lose this fight, I'll slice my own throat before I let these monsters touch me.

Before he can even push his pants down, I

lunge at him, blade poised. The asshole pivots out of my path, lashing out and grabbing my blade-wielding hand, squeezing until I cry with pain.

The weapon drops from my grasp and he snatches my throat. "You will be fun to break, wild bitch."

"Fuck you." I spit in his face.

He raises a hand and strikes me hard across the cheek, the pain reverberating up the side of my skull. White stars dance behind my eyes as the world tilts on its axis.

One second he's there, the next he's ripped away, and I'm stumbling to catch my balance.

Growls and shouts deafen me. Panic crashes into me as I rub my eyes to see clearly again. Air buffets against me from the commotion. The wolves behind me whimper, and they're gone in seconds. I lower my hand from my face where it still burns, and in front of me stands Dušan in wolf form, blood dripping from his mouth. At his feet lies the bearded man, unmoving, with a gaping hole in his chest, like Dušan has broken right through his ribs to tear out his heart.

The bloody image should terrify me, but I've never felt so protected in my life. To see him go to such extremes toward anyone who hurt me makes my stomach flutter.

He's transforming, and within moments he stands before me as a man, his body cut and bleeding. But I rush into his arms, regardless.

Around my Alphas, I feel at home. I can't even make sense of that thought, but it's the truth.

I finally pull away as Lucien joins us, naked and battered, but smirking. "Well, that was fun." He laughs and wipes at the bleeding cut on his lip.

A shadow of a wolf darts amid the trees in the distance, chased by another. A strangled cry of pain floods the woods.

"What's going on? Is Bardhyl all right?"

As if answering my call, he races across the woods directly past us, his white fur matted and stained with blood. He's bigger than I remember him, teeth bared, and there isn't a hint of humanity in his eyes. He vanishes into the shadows, and another scream rings in the air.

"Bardhyl lost himself to the fight, so we're letting him clean up the rest so his Berserker can get it out of his system."

I blink in the direction he vanished, and I won't deny that seeing him that way scares me. He's taking down the rest of the pack on his own? "How often does he get like this?"

"When he's so angry, he can't hold back," Lucien answers.

"What do we do?" I ask. "And what about Evan?"

"Evan will never hurt anyone again, babe. Now we sit and wait for Bardhyl to finish off the pack. Then we try to calm him down."

That part sounds terrifying. I don't know how much time passes before Bardhyl reappears, still in his wolf form. He's breathing heavily, blood splashed over his long, pointy nose. His chest heaves in and out, his lips peeling back, his ears flat to his head.

A shiver races up my spine and buckles my knees. He's staring straight at me, and behind those eyes, there's no sign of Bardhyl. "Umm, guys, what is he doing?"

Then he lunges at us.

CHAPTER 15

MEIRA

’m lost to fear, staring at the white wolf lunging right at me.

My legs won’t move. My scream wedges in my throat.

There’s no sign of Bardhyl in those deep, green eyes. Just his wild animal side.

Lucien drives a hand across my stomach and shoves me behind him, while he and Dušan intercept.

They leap at the wolf, each colliding into Bardhyl.

I retreat, my heart about to give out as the three of them land in a great heap. An explosion of growls pierces the air, the wolf’s teeth snapping, his lips peeled back.

Bardhyl growls, and he never once takes his eyes off me—like I'm his meal and he'll kill anything in his path to reach me. Dušan locks an arm around his neck, while Lucien throws himself on top of him.

This isn't Bardhyl. Not my Bardhyl… the man who drove me crazy in the cave, who made me fall for him. How can he be my fated mate when he looks ready to kill me?

He's a monster.

Uncontrollable.

Savage.

Dušan and Lucien have him pinned to the ground, while a thunderous threat snarls through him.

"Meira!" Dušan yells. "Come over here."

I scoff and recoil further. "That's never going to happen. Look at him."

"*Meira*," he growls. "He seeks a connection with you to calm him and push back the wolf."

I blink hard at both of them straining to hold down the wild wolf. He wants me to *pat* him? "He's going to bite my arm off, isn't he?"

"We won't let that happen, but hurry the hell up."

Lucien glances up at me, his jawline tight,

fighting with all his might to keep Bardhyl down. "He needs you."

Oh, geez, I'm doing this, aren't I? I step forward and lick my dried lips, my arms stiff by my side. The closer I get, the fiercer Bardhyl thrashes and growls. Does he know what we're doing, or will that come after he eats me?

I sidestep around them, giving Bardhyl's head a wide berth. His eyes follow me as I reach his side. My arms shake as I stretch them out and run my fingers through his thick, lush fur. It's knotted with blood, and his body is vibrating and scorching hot.

He thrusts, and with the touch comes an electric zap that jolts up my arms.

I flinch back just as Bardhyl bucks the other Alphas off him. A split second is all it takes for him to bite me.

I scream, my body numbing, and all I see is my end.

His head strikes my chest, bowling me over, and I yell from the pain. Then the ass leaps over me and into the woods. I cry out, clutching a hand to where he knocked into me.

I tilt my head back all the way to watch him vanishing into the shadows.

Dušan grabs my arms and has me on my feet in moments. He holds me close with one hand, pulling twigs out of my hair with the other.

"What the hell was that?" I snap. "You said you had a hold of him."

"Once you touched him, he wasn't going to hurt you," Dušan explains while Lucien joins us, dusting himself off.

"You could have said that earlier, you know. I'm pretty sure I just had my first heart attack."

Lucien smirks at me. "You're so dramatic. We had him under control. You think we haven't dealt with him like this before?"

"Well, *I* haven't." I pull myself out of Dušan's hold, breathing slowly to calm my pulse and chase away the fear strangling me. "So where is he now? Will he come back as himself?"

"He needs time to recover," Dušan explains. "He's a Berserker at heart, Meira. Something horrible happened to him and his pack back in Denmark, and the scar of the atrocity turned his wolf into a wild creature that even he sometimes struggles to control."

I swallow past the boulder in my throat. What have I gotten myself into? "Will he be okay out there alone?" I ask. I'd be lying if I said I'm not intimidated or a bit frightened by him, but what blossomed between us last night pulses just as hard in my chest now.

The crunch of foliage has me lifting my head as Lucien returns, dressed and holding clothes that he hands over to his Alpha. With everything happening, it's only now that I really full paid attention Dušan's nudity. The strong expanse of his muscles cut sharply across his chest, abs, and arms. Messy, dark hair hangs over his shoulders and face as he bends forward to step into his pants. I can't stop my eyes from looking at his cock, how perfect it is, how I remember him claiming me, knotting inside me. Everything about him—about all my Alphas—is beyond sexy. They're achingly beautiful, these men who have monsters living inside them… as do I, if we can ever manage to bring her out.

When Dušan catches me staring, the corners of his mouth quirk in a devilish grin, his eyes holding a silent promise of what's to come. "Let's move. We'll spend the night in the cottage by the river." He presses his lips together and glances over to Lucien. Without words, Lucien nods and goes in the opposite direction.

"Where's he going?" I look out after him.

"To find food. We won't make it back home by dark, and I want to wait for Bardhyl."

Warmth curls in my belly. Dušan cares for those close to him, and that I admire about him. In this world, no one gives a shit about others. Maybe that's why he has such a large pack, why they stay and fight for him. I reach up and pull a leaf out of his hair. He grabs my hand and brings it to his mouth. The kiss sends small sparks up my arm and through my body. Something in his blue eyes flickers, like he feels the sensation as well.

"Are you hurt?" he asks as he draws me toward him, holding me so near, I feel his erection. Hell, that is fast.

His fingers carefully comb through my messy hair. His scent, masculine and dark, is savage and washes over my senses. Shudders travel through me as his other hand crawls under my top and cups a breast, his fingers pinching my nipple.

I cry out with desire.

"Never run away from me again. We are one. And you are mine."

My panties melt in moments, and my body has no control when it comes to these wolves. His dominance is an aphrodisiac.

I pant against him, staring at his full lips,

picturing them dragging down my body, pressed against my slit. One minute I'm scared for my life, the next I want to jump Dušan. That seems to be normal for me around these Alphas.

"I will never lose you again," he snarls and swallows loudly, the tendons in his throat moving as he speaks. "I will go into the afterlife itself to collect you if you die on me."

Dušan

Her gaze widens.

I mean every damn word. These past few days have been torture. When I look into her pale, bronze eyes now, I see a woman who no longer resembles the lost girl I first found in the woods. She's changed, grown braver, started to find herself.

I lower my head and take a whiff of her sweet scent of cherries, her ruby lips parting expectantly. I squeeze her breast, her nipple pebbled tightly... so damn perfect. My cock twitches in my pants, hardening. Does she even realize what impact she has on me… on all of us? I never truly understood the connection between fated mates, even when Lucien explained it and I witnessed his excruciating agony. Nothing prepared me for the force that now wreaks havoc on my heart.

She looks up at me, her fingers curling around the fabric of my long-sleeved tee, and grinds her body against me. Our lips melt together. Heat and sweetness fill me when her tongue curls with mine. I draw her closer and kiss her back deeply, drowning in her growing slick scent that has my groin pulsing. I drive my hardness against her, and she moans in my mouth. My heart pounds faster.

Fuck, I've missed her. All I can picture is stripping her and taking her against a tree. Before I can stop myself, I walk her back, pinning her against a trunk, and plaster myself against her small form.

I was hers first, and she will always be mine. Gorgeous and fiery. But fucking her now isn't going to work. We're out in the open and in dangerous territory.

"You do such things to me," she breathes. "My body responds in ways I can't understand." She kisses me again, thrusting her breasts against my chest. Then her hand lowers and slides into the front of my pants. She grasps my cock, and I hiss with desperate need.

"Take me," she begs, and it drives me wild. Her mouth is on mine again, and she's biting my lips, her scent engulfing me, drowning me.

I tear my mouth from hers with all the inner strength I have. "Not here, Meira. When I fuck you, I will take my time, make you scream."

She protests with a groan that drives me insane, then she falls to her knees before me. Her hunger shudders me to the core as I struggle to hold mine back. I shouldn't have started this, because one touch awakens the savage essence that brings an Omega and Alpha together. Her need grows.

Her fingers pull at my pants, unbuttoning them, and my cock springs out, so fucking erect it aches.

I should say *no*, but the irresistible desire pushes and pushes me.

Those gorgeous, sexy lips slide down over the tip of my cock, and I'm gone. Her warm mouth is like wildfire and her tongue flicks me, licking me, sucking me harder.

I growl, my wolf roaring within me. I plant a hand on the tree behind her as she draws me deeper and hold my other hand to the back of her head, guiding her.

I twitch under her mercy, my gaze trained on her as she glances up at me with intensity in her eyes, as her mouth glides back and forth over me. Just seeing her claiming me has blood rushing to my dick.

Deep down, sizzling sparks mingle with my lust.

Tonight, I will fuck her... and that's if I can make it to the cottage without plunging my cock into her sweet, tight pussy first.

She sucks me harder and I howl, the pleasure thrumming over me with the ferocity of a storm. Thank the universe, wolves' cocks only knot when fucking, not during blow jobs, because I'd be pissed as hell if I couldn't enjoy this.

I groan louder and I want this to last... which is a problem out here. We're sitting targets while I get off.

Goddammit.

I slip out of her gorgeous mouth, and she stares up at me with pleading eyes.

"Don't look at me that way. I'm barely holding on." I collect her hand and help her to her feet, then button myself up. My cock is a fucking anaconda and barely fits in my pants in its current state.

"Please, Dušan."

I cup her cheeks and kiss her sweet lips. "That was sexy as hell, but we must get to safety first. Dusk is approaching, and we need to find shelter."

I glance over my shoulder. It's too quiet. Nerves crawl up my spine as I picture the undead coming at us.

She gives me a single nod, and the lust claiming both of us eases with the cold breeze washing past.

I lead her through the woods and to the old cottage by the river, picking up sticks on the way in the hopes that Lucien brings back an abundant catch.

"I missed you," Meira murmurs.

I squeeze her hand in mine gently and glance over to her as she smiles at me. She may not say it, but this is the closest I will get to her apologizing for running away. And I am okay with that.

CHAPTER 16

MEIRA

The door to the small cottage creaks as Dušan pushes it open. A stale, musty odor greets us. I cringe and stare into the darkness inside. Dušan enters first, the wooden floorboards groaning under each step he takes. He walks to the fireplace and dumps the armful of wood he collected. I grip my bundle, waiting at the doorway. As he vanishes into a corridor, I glance behind us. There's no sign of Lucien, who's hunting for food, and I have no idea where Bardhyl went.

Returning moments later, Dušan waves me in. "All safe."

Then he throws open the ancient yellow

curtains decorated with small red chilis and creates a plume of dust in the air.

I cough. "This place has mountains of dirt."

I head inside, set my collection of timber near the fireplace, and help him open the windows to freshen up the air. The main room has one long couch positioned in front of an oversized, old-style fireplace housing a cauldron hanging from a metal hook. Several chairs are on their side in a corner, and that's it. No other furniture. The place seems lonely, barren, and sad. Walls are bare of images or any sign of the family who once lived here. Whoever they were, they had time to pack and leave after the curse took hold. I find a broom and start sweeping the floor clean of dust so I don't sneeze all night. Plus, once night falls, we'll need to close the windows and curtains to avoid getting the undead's attention from a distance with flickering light.

Dušan enters the room with his arms full of blankets and towels. "Look what I found in the closet. They'll keep us warm." He heaps them onto the couch, and I quickly grab the one that looks to be the largest and cover the couch with it.

He heads outside and returns with a bucket of water. "Sit down. Let me clean your bite mark."

"It should heal quick enough on its own," I say, but I still sit down on the couch.

He flops down next to me with a wet rag as I drag my top down over my shoulder to reveal the wound. Blood smudges my skin and sticks to the fabric. Gently, he wipes the blood away, focusing intently on what he's doing.

"Thanks for coming for me, for protecting me, for tending to me. I'm not really used to someone being so…" I can't think of the right word.

"Loving, caring, incredibly amazing?" he jokes.

I mean to laugh, but the rawness of the mark stings and I wince instead. Looking over to my shoulder, I see there are four clear punctures and several smaller teeth indentations. A perfect bite mark.

"Does it hurt a lot?" he asks.

"It's not the first time I've been bitten. Won't be the last, I'm sure."

He wipes the bubbling drop of blood and places the fabric against the injury, applying pressure until the blood coagulates. "From now on, the only bites you'll receive are from us three." There's burning fire behind his gaze, and my mind goes back to the woods when I took him into my mouth. I've never done that before, but it felt natural, and the hunger inside me for him was unlike anything I'd experienced. It's stronger than before. Just the thought of it has a pulse dancing between my thighs.

As if sensing the sexual craving growing inside me, Dušan's eyes widen, and I catch the skip of his breath. He's on his feet in moments. "Let me get the fire started. Go and see what you can find in the other rooms that we can use."

When he pulls away, my fingers tingle to reach over and draw him to my side. A burning intoxication crawls over me, and maybe he's right. I ought to distract myself with something else before we end up rutting and Lucien returns with our meal to find we've done nothing else.

Dušan wastes no time and kneels in front of the fireplace, getting set to light it.

Up on my feet, I lick my lips and ignore the growing itch to kiss him, then head into the kitchen. The cupboards are empty. There are only a handful of plates, some cutlery and even some candles scattered in the drawers. No oven. I wander down the dark hallway and into a gritty bathroom. The stink makes me gag when I spot the dead rat in the shower, so I shut the door quickly. The next room has a single wire bed, no mattress, with rags and paper tossed about on the floor.

The last room offers a large bed and even a standalone wardrobe. I peel back the curtains and cough from the dust it stirs in the air. Outside is a perfect view of the river about twenty feet away, water splashing against the rocks along the bank, and beyond that lies the forest. It almost looks tranquil, which is completely deceitful.

Hastily, I check the wardrobe that smells like mothballs. No clothes or shoes, but at the base I find more blankets. They're blue, my favorite color, so I snatch them up and spread one out on the bed. Then I throw myself into it and smile.

For years, I slept on the wooden floor of my treehouse, or on branches in trees, so this is utter heaven just as it had been on the beds in the Ash Wolves compound.

The mattress indents near my legs. My heart skips a beat, and I jerk around, only to come face-to-face with Dušan.

Prowling, he crawls over me while I remain on my stomach, his blue gaze finding mine. This Alpha is a warrior, a leader, a survivor. He has so many following him, in awe of his beliefs, and I admire that about him. It seems impossible that such a man would be here with me now, looking at me like I'm already naked and he's not releasing me until he stakes his claim.

He's on all fours over me, and his fingers scrape over my neck as he brushes my hair aside. Hot lips find the tenderness of my neck, his breath on fire, while his erection settles against the curve of my ass.

"For days, I've been thinking about fucking you," he whispers in my ear, leaving me shaking with arousal.

It doesn't take much for him to turn me on. A kiss, a touch, a few words, and I'm putty in his hands.

"Would you like that?" His weight lifts off me, and his hands are on the band of my pants. He rips them off me instantly, jerking my whole body from his aggressiveness. A hard slap connects with my ass.

I wince and glance over my shoulder at him. But his eyes are glued to my ass, his hands on his belt, pulling at the buckle.

He rewards me with a sinful grin filled with his intentions. A simple look and I'm shivering with the excitement building within me.

"Back in the woods, you undid me," he says,

lifting his gaze to mine. "You make me feel things no one ever has."

His words are fierce and strong. Our first time together, he was gentler with me, more patient, but the man before me is too far gone to do anything but rut me. And I find it sexy as hell that I make him lose control.

"Up on your hands and knees," he orders. He captures my hips and lifts them.

I obey him as his hand slides between my thighs to part my legs. Greedy fingers slip over the seam of my pussy, soft at first, then with two fingers, he pries apart my lips, his touch grazing over swollen, tender flesh.

I still, my heart racing as I draw in a rushed breath.

His touch comes again, sliding across my slick heat that coats the inside of my thighs. He consumes me with his mere presence. He pushes two fingers into me, thrusting hard and urgently. I arch my back, loving the euphoria, and buck back against him. Then he draws them out and climbs off the bed.

I wrench my head around, but he shakes his finger at me. "I never said you could move. Stay right there where I can see your juicy offering waiting for me."

My core clenches at hearing his words, and he laughs like he sees the impact he has on me.

He strips off his pants and shirt, standing at the foot of the bed, naked and captivating.

"Your pussy is sexy as fuck."

Those have to be the most beautiful words in the English language.

He is mine and I am his… Those are the words going through my mind as my body burns for him. He's back, kneeling behind me, his fingers slipping up my back and twisting my hair around his hand. Gently, he tugs my head back as the tip of his cock nudges at my entrance.

He growls savagely, and my body responds, pulsing with adrenaline, my inner walls already sucking onto his dick.

My heart racing, I moan as he pushes into me, one hand pulling on my hair, the other grasping my hip. He drives deep, powerful and dominating.

I cry out with the arousal flaring over me, tearing through me with unbearable need. He fucks me hard, and I rock my pelvis back and forth to meet his. The bedsprings creak, the metal headboard hitting the wall.

He claims me, reminding us both of what he's missed, what he thought he lost.

My moans of pleasure escape as he thrusts deeper, his own growls thunderous. Letting go of my hair, he grips my hips, fingers digging into flesh, and he pumps, losing himself in me.

Fiery desire and sexual lust burn between us. His strength overpowers me, and I let him take me, opening myself up, wanting my wolf to connect with his. We are steeped in sex and fear that what we have will be ripped from us.

His cock grows within me, the tip swelling as he ruts me.

It's the perfect way he fucks me. I've wanted to hide from him from the beginning, to run away, but I've been wrong. He's the answer to everything I never knew I wanted.

"Don't you leave again..." he murmurs, the sound barely audible, but I hear it along with agony in his voice. It's why he's taking me so roughly, why he's on the edge of losing himself. This is his punishment to me for making him suffer. I get it, and I should be pissed, but all I see is a man who's struggling with unfamiliar emotions.

I moan with each thrust, my hands clutching the blanket, my toes curling. Rapture soars so fast across me that the room starts spinning. My nipples are so tight, they ache. He reaches around my waist and dips down to my clit, rubbing it. Arousal ignites as if it'd been waiting there for the trigger, and fuck... I scream with the orgasm tearing through me, shaking me, hurling me into the heavens and making me forget everything.

The climax makes me clench down on everything.

Dušan growls as I tighten around his cock, and he thrusts faster.

Suddenly, he stills as he roars, spilling his seed inside me. There's so much of it. I feel its warmth, crave it, need it. I gasp for air when my body finally buckles with exhaustion, and I drop face-first, flat on the bed with Dušan on top of me. Both of us are gasping for air, our bodies sweaty and hearts racing. He reaches down over my chin, forcing me to face him, then his mouth claims mine in a scorching kiss.

He's buried deep inside me, locked within me with his cock knotted. It's everything I crave. Part of me keeps thinking that he, Lucien, and Bardhyl don't deserve a complication like me. That I will only bring sorrow to their lives. But I remind myself it's much too late now. Those thoughts are from the past me. We've come so far, our connection solidifying with every passing second we spend together. The new me wants to embrace change, to recognize that being on my own is no longer an option.

Dusan breaks our kiss and rolls us onto our sides, his arms wrapped around the front of my shoulders and stomach.

Our breaths ease, and I melt back against his chest, his passion pulling at my emotions for him.

"Don't you leave again."

His words sing over my mind. It never occurred to me that my absence would affect the Alphas this much.

His lips brush my ear. "I couldn't resist when I saw you lying on the bed."

"I craved that release," I admit. After the pent-up desire in the woods, I needed this more than I even realized.

He holds me and I close my eyes, letting myself pretend we're safe in his compound. A gentle heat spreads over my chest in his presence, and I sense my wolf stirring there, like she's trapped inside and doesn't know how to come out. Well, that makes two of us.

"Can you feel your wolf?" he asks me, placing a

palm flat against my chest. "I sensed her trying to come out when we were as one."

"Yeah, for the first time, I really do. Like she's humming just below the surface, but she feels lost."

"I remember her trying to reach out to my wolf. That's progress, Meira. I never felt her like this the first time we were together."

I smile and grasp onto his strong arm around me, believing that there may be hope enough for me to somehow come out of all this surviving. It's odd after all this time I've longed to not be found, for others to leave me alone, for the world to take me if it wished. Loneliness does strange things to one's mind. But now, all I wish for is to not lose my life. And it has everything to do with what my three Alphas are offering me.

They are mine. I claimed them as much as they did me, and the universe can go fuck itself if it thinks it will get in our way. Though the trepidation doesn't leave me entirely. It's there at the back of my mind, constantly reminding me of my terminal sickness and the fear that if I do finally shift, my wolf will go mad and kill me and those I love.

Lucien

 ight has begun to steal the day by the time I head down the hill to the dilapidated cottage near the water. I found it earlier, the hut having doors and windows intact, so I'm hopeful that no one will come crashing in here while we sleep. After the attack from that dickhead Evan, I contemplated the idea of us traveling through the night to get home already. But it's better we rest for the night and leave first thing in the morning. My stomach clenches at the memory of the fight. I wanted to be the one to rip Evan's head off, but Dušan finishing him off felt just as damn good.

Now, I head back to cottage with two rabbits and one pheasant that took longer than I anticipated to catch, as animals aren't so readily available these days. But they'll feed us, and I'd bet one of my legs that Bardhyl has already gorged on whatever he tracked in the woods to exhaust his wolf's adrenaline. More rabbit for me. I pick at my teeth, trying to remove the bit of fur still wedged in them from when I chased these critters in wolf form. One or two might have accidentally been eaten raw.

I stroll over to the single-story house. The weathered wooden walls have splinters of wood peeling away from the surface, the roof is rusty, and wild grass and weeds suffocate the landscape. Smoke curls out of the chimney, so that means Dušan and Meira are already here and ready for a meal.

The reality that we finally found Meira and she's ours still has my stomach bursting with excitement. I don't know what I would have done if we'd lost her in the woods.

I glance over my shoulder and find no undead following. Good. There's an old bench by the side of the house, where I dump the kills. Then I grab a wooden bucket and I fill it with water from the river. When I return and take a seat, I skin the rabbits and prepare them for roasting.

The front door creaks open, and Meira peers around the corner, staring at me in surprise. Her hair is wet and her cheeks rosy, like she's gone for a dip in the river. "Thought I heard the sound of the gruesome act of skinning." She smirks at her own sarcasm, and I adore that she can still make jokes after everything we've gone through today.

"Make yourself useful." I reach over and hand her the pheasant.

She sits on the opposite end of the bench, barely an arm's length away. She takes the animal into her lap and without hesitation begins plucking it. I notice the slight droop in one of her shoulders from where she was bitten by that asswipe Evan. It's creeps like that who have ruined our world.

"Dušan's preparing a spit, and there's a cauldron in the fireplace. He's making a soup with wild onions and mushrooms he found, and he's just waiting for the meat." She pauses for a moment, focusing on cleaning the bird. "You think witches once lived here?" There's mirth in her voice. "I mean, who uses a cauldron for cooking, right?" She snickers to herself, and there's a new energy around her, like she's slept and woken up rejuvenated.

And just as I have the thought, the answer comes to me. She's high on adrenaline, and when the breeze brushes past me, I inhale her scent, her heat...and also Dušan's. Whatever happened between them has taken the edge off her.

That's the thing... an Alpha's influence over an Omega is more than just satisfaction of a sexual craving for breeding. It helps stabilize emotions, which many Omegas don't realize.

"The last thing we want in this world are powerful witches who can turn us all into frogs." I laugh at the image in my mind.

"Maybe having witches in charge wouldn't be so bad. The undead would be dealt with, for one thing." She plucks at the feathers and throws them on the grass, making the place look like a chicken slaughterhouse.

"So you think the biggest problem in this world is the undead?" I ask.

Her head tilts to look over at me. "Well, yeah, you don't agree? The virus destroyed the world, and now it's unsafe to go anywhere."

"There are worse things out there than the undead, gorgeous. Alphas who slay anyone in sight, who imprison women for breeding… those kinds of wolves are multiplying, and *they* are the real plague making this world worse. Eradicate the warlords and we stand a chance to bring back some sense of community and humanity to our world."

"Wow, that's kind of deep." She twists toward me, drawing a bent knee up on the bench between us. "You, Dušan, and Bardhyl aren't like other men I've encountered. Why?"

I rip the last bit of fur off the rabbit's leg with a tug. "Dušan's belief that we can change the world for the better has rubbed off on us."

"You trust him with your life, don't you?"

I nod. "Of course. He saved me from the undead when I was young, and I pledged myself to him ever since. There hasn't been a day where I regretted that decision."

She goes quiet for a moment and keeps plucking the pheasant until it's almost clean of feathers, except for the head. "I'm sorry about what happened with your first mate." She looks down at the plucked bird. "Since all this, the feelings I have are so overwhelming that they seem to control me. So I can only imagine how it must have felt when you lost your fated partner."

"It's okay. Life takes and it gives again. I accept that," I answer almost immediately. I've had many people ask me this question, and my response comes out automated. "But I think I refused to let myself get over her… and used that as a reason to not be with anyone else on a serious level. I mean, wolves can be together even if not fated mates, but it always felt like I'd be cheating on her."

Meira places her clean bird next to my two skinned rabbits. "Lucien, I don't…" She licks her lips and looks at me like she's trying to find her words. "I don't want to be the next reason you don't want to find love again."

It takes me a split second to work out she's referring to dying from her sickness. The thought turns my stomach sour, the feeling pouring through my veins at what I've been through once already.

"I refuse to think of the worst-case scenario, Meira. Otherwise, I'd never get out of bed most mornings. We found each other for a reason, and I sure as fuck am not going to sit around and just lose you. Once we get back home, we'll talk to our medics and work this out." Threads of desperation seep into my voice, and I hate sounding weak.

She reaches over, her small fingers curling over mine. "I ran away from you all because I would rather have you hate me for leaving than have you feel guilty when you couldn't save me. Or be responsible for your deaths if my wolf rips out and slaughters you." Her eyes glisten, and fuck, my chest tightens. She did it for us, and it's in this moment that I see how deeply she has fallen for us as well. Even if she keeps fighting us, I know that comes from fear, not hate. Fear for our safety. Fear of what we could have. Fear of what we could lose.

"Meira, I'd rather have a few weeks with you than none at all."

Her chin suddenly trembles, and tears drench her cheeks. *Shit.* I'm on my feet and I draw her into my arms. "Don't cry. We'll find a cure, I promise you."

She glances up, and I wipe away a loose tear. "It's not me I'm crying for, but the pain I'll cause you three if I can't get my wolf out."

"There's only one solution then." I tuck a bent finger under her chin. "We get that goddamn wolf to come out, even if we have to lock ourselves in a bedroom for the next few weeks."

She laughs and I embrace her, my heart squeezing at the trepidation hanging over us at the thought that she might not heal. Fuck, I hate those thoughts.

She draws back and smiles, her eyes glinting in the descending sun. Her irises seem to almost glow in the reddish light, and her cheery smile desperately tugs at my heart. I reach over and twirl a finger in her dark hair.

"If you keep looking at me that way, we'll never

make it inside," she teases, a tiny dimple appearing when she smiles so deeply.

"And that's a bad thing, why?"

She raises her shoulders. "Never said it was bad, just that we'd never make it inside."

Dušan steps around the corner of the house, carrying a bucket, and pauses when he finds us. "Hell, I'm starving. Bring those inside," he growls and tosses me the wooden pail. "Make yourself handy and bring in more water for the soup and tea. We can make some with the mint I found."

I laugh and stroll down to the river. When I glance back, Dušan leans a shoulder against the wall of the house, studying Meira as she collects the rabbits and pheasant. He's completely lost, as much as me, when it comes to her.

After losing Cataline, my heartbreaking agony left me useless and shattered. So gods help the whole pack if Meira doesn't survive, because Dušan won't know what will have hit him. Her survival has become about so much more than just her and us now…

If Dušan goes down, so will the pack.

CHAPTER 17

MEIRA

$\mathcal{I}$ can't remember the last time I felt so
sated, so warm, so content. Lucien
lounges on the floor in front of the fire like he's a
cat all stretched out with his belly full of food,
while Dušan sits near me on the couch, my feet in
his lap and his magical fingers pressing in all the
right spots on my soles.

"If you just gave me this massage the first time
we met in the woods, Dušan, I would never have
run away." I giggle at my silliness, and Lucien looks
over at us, rolling his eyes.

"If only it were that easy, my little hellcat,"
Dušan says, laughing.

Lucien just looks at me with mischief.

The fire's blaze is a blanket around me, and it

has me ready to sleep out here rather than back in the bedroom. I look toward the door, then turn to Dušan. "Do you think Bardhyl is okay out there alone?"

"In his current state he is, and there's nothing we can do for him until he calms down."

Lucien lies on his back on the blanket spread over the wooden floorboards to resemble a rug in front of the fire. "Last year, he was gone for three days and came back completely shaved, head and body."

"What happened?"

Lucien pushes himself to his ass and turns to us, already laughing. Dušan starts chuckling at whatever memory they've both recalled.

"It's only funny if you share it with me too," I explain, my gaze flipping from one guy to the other.

"Well, he slipped and fell down a gorge and landed in a patch of poison ivy," Lucien begins. "He itched like crazy, so much so that he ended up passing out right outside a small gated community for humans." He breaks out into hysterical laughter, while I'm still waiting for the punchline.

Dušan takes over. "Two girls, who were seventeen or eighteen, according to Bardhyl, found him naked in human form and red from itching. They thought he was a human like them and had been attacked, so they dragged him into their home and shaved his whole body, including his head, insisting he had fleas and they couldn't let them infest their house."

My mouth drops open. "They shaved him *everywhere?*" I emphasize the last word.

Lucien howls with laughter, happy tears dripping from his eyes. "Get this. They carved a heart in his pubes."

I can't hold back this time as I picture this powerful, Viking wolf completely bald and shaved, except for the heart over his groin. My stomach hurts from laughing so much, as I can just imagine how mad he must have been.

When I can't laugh anymore because it hurts too much, I slouch on the couch and wipe away my tears. "Oh my god, that is hilarious. He would have been so pissed off."

"He woke up and startled the girls, who screamed that he was a fleabag, then he bolted out of there, realizing he'd been shaved. We never let him live it down. It took him a long time to grow his hair back," Lucien says.

"And it's why he vows to never cut it again," Dušan murmurs.

"Poor guy. But I bet those girls had fun shaving a huge hunk of a man, and they would have *so* touched his large cock."

I smirk at the image in my head because I probably would have, too, out of curiosity.

Both men look at me strangely then. "What?"

"He was probably flaccid," Lucien points out, and I arch a brow. *This* is the part they're hung up on? Really?

"If it makes you feel better, I think you're all damn large," I say. "I've only seen a few here and there, and well, you three are packing incredible weapons."

Lucien gets to his knees and pulls at his buckle. "I think she wants us to compare for her. What do you say, Dušan?"

"No, that's not what I said. Geez, keep it in your pants." I roll my eyes hard at them, but it suddenly feels like an inferno in the cabin.

Dušan chuckles at us, and I am convinced my cheeks are burning up bright red.

"Fine. When Bardhyl returns, we'll line up for you. Then you'll see I'm the winner," Lucien says.

Dušan clears his throat.

I push up and off of the couch. "I'll leave it to you two to sort it out, and maybe you can get me a hot cup of tea while you're at it."

While my first option is to head outside to go to the toilet, I have second thoughts and instead head to the rat-stinky one in the house. I sure as hell don't want to be surprised out there while peeing, and more than likely, Dušan or Lucien would insist on joining me and probably watching.

The bathroom reeks so bad, stinging my nostrils with the pungent smell like spoiled eggs, and it really couldn't be from one rat, but for all I know there are half a dozen more in the walls. A small candle I found earlier in a kitchen drawer now sits on the dirty sink, the flame flickering and throwing shadows over the walls.

I stare down at the filthy toilet bowl. I doubt the flush is working, but I only need to pee, so that will be fine. Quickly, I get it over and done with, the whole time my gaze hovering on the rat. What killed him anyway? Starvation? There are no flies buzzing around, so it probably died a while ago.

In no time, I'm finished and out of the room, spotting Dušan and Lucien laughing as they head out the front door. "Fuck, I need to piss so much," Lucien mutters.

I roll my eyes and head into the main bedroom to grab another blanket, as it's getting cold, even with the fire.

Back in the main room, I stroll toward the couch when movement in a shadow by the door startles me, and I jump in my skin. A small squeal escapes my lips. "I swear to god, Lucien, if that's you, I'm going to skin you alive for scaring me."

My blade is in my boots near the fireplace, and I frantically scan for a weapon within reach when the figure steps forward into the fire's light.

Bardhyl.

He's naked.

Has a feral expression on his face.

His green eyes are locked on me.

On the bright side, he's no longer in his wolf form, though he still seems dangerous, even if alluring. My feelings are at war with my desire for him.

"Oh! When did you get back?" I glance over to the door, figuring I can make a run for it—or, better yet, scream—if Bardhyl makes a move.

He tilts his head to the side just like an animal might do, and this time, the fright crawls up my spine.

"We left you food."

He looks over to the cauldron. Okay, so he understands my words.

"Bardhyl, you're scaring me," I admit.

He comes to me with such speed, I don't have time to react. He drives into me, my back hitting the wall, his mouth on mine, stealing my scream.

Still on edge, I'm trying to make sense of which Bardhyl this is… the crazed wolf or the dominant one.

But as much as my own arousal flares in response and turns to liquid between my thighs, I don't want to become his prey. What if he can't tell the difference between sex and a meal?

I break from his kiss. "Bardhyl, stop." I stomp my heel on his foot.

He hisses, giving me enough space to slip out from him and rush down the corridor. Fuck, of course I'd go the wrong way. I dart into the bedroom.

Bardhyl charges in after me, clenching his jaw. The candle perched up on the cupboard illuminates him and reveals the hunger in his eyes for me.

My body betrays me, craving him and thrumming, which is so wrong. He's an animal, I see it in his eyes, and I'm struggling between going to him to calm him down and jumping out the window.

"Meira," he growls, so dark and heavy, and my body responds with a fluttering in my stomach. Really, wolf, you want him while he's in crazy Berserker mode?

"Bardhyl… this isn't you. Let's talk about it a bit first."

He shakes his head and is on me in seconds, pinning me to the wall. His mouth is on my neck, and he licks me from my collarbone to my earlobe.

I shouldn't find this arousing when I'm shaking with fear, but the more he licks me, the hotter I burn. Callused fingers graze under my top, and he rips it up and over my head, my arms forced up as he strips me with ease.

Fuck. I'm breathing heavily, my clit throbbing as he shoves my pants down my legs. By the time he's bent over and has pulled them off my ankles, I've collected myself and knee him in the chin. He stumbles, groaning as I leap past him, sprinting toward the door.

Strong hands snatch my wrist. I spin around to face one of my fated mates, the wolf who loves to toy around and do deals so he wins, who flirts with me and now looks ready to mount me. I'm battling between *fuck yeah* and *this is moving too fast* after seeing him lose himself in the woods.

Our bodies collide, and his large hand scoops me up by my ass, the tips of his fingers reaching the heat of my pussy. I moan from the touch almost instantly, like I'm programmed to respond to him. As though control is a thing of the past when it comes to me and these Alphas.

"Bardhyl, please, let's just take it slow." Not that it's what my body wants, but I'm not too sure what will happen if I just let him take the lead.

He looks at me, licking his lips, then shoves me onto the bed.

I land on my back and bounce, the springs groaning beneath me. Swiftly, he snatches me by the back of my knees, draws me to the edge of the bed, and spreads my legs. I push forward and shove my hand against his head while trying to shuffle away.

"Be still," he snarls, and his mouth assaults my pussy. He dives in and latches on to my lips, taking all of me.

A shudder races up my spine, and if I thought I was aroused before, now I'm a puddle, melting before him.

He frantically licks me, and god, he has a wide

and long tongue. The moment he plunges it into my slit, I arch my back and scream with desire. He shoves my legs wider, eating me savagely. The wet, slurping sounds he makes should be illegal.

I writhe beneath him, drowning in pleasure, when I should be using the moment to get away from him. Though now I'm more torn about why I wanted to get away from him in the first place. My thoughts spin while I cry out from him tugging on my burning lips, the sensation driving me insane. My eyes are shut, and I can't think straight or even care right now that Bardhyl's beast side is claiming me.

I reach down and fist his hair, pushing his face on my pussy as I grind against him. His fingers dig into my inner thighs. He's loving every moment.

"Fuck me!" Lucien snarls.

My eyes flip open to find him and Dušan there, both of them with their hands on their cocks, watching Bardhyl go to town on me. Where the hell have they been… or have they been watching this the whole time?

He releases me and I collapse on my back, shyly pressing my knees together, which is crazy.

"How long have you two been watching?" I ask as I shuffle farther up on the bed, drawing my knees to my chest, the pillow at my back. I'm humming with an orgasm just under the surface. My arousal coats the inside of my thighs, and I'm close to drooling.

"Long enough," Dušan answers, his voice raspy, his eyes already glazed over with lust.

"And you were okay with him attacking me while being controlled by his wolf?"

Lucien shrugs. "You seemed to be having fun." He turns to Bardhyl. "When'd you get back, man?"

"Earlier. Popped in to find the house empty at first."

Rage rises through me. "What the hell? So you're not out of control?"

Bardhyl glances over and winks at me. "Oh, cupcake, it's just a little payback for tying me up in the cave."

My mouth drops open at the revelation that he did all that as revenge. I snatch the pillow at my back and toss it at him, hitting him square in the chest. "You bastard."

"And you, my sweet cherry pie, are a horny little girl with the most perfect and sweetest pussy in the world."

I'm lost for words, not sure what to say. I throw him a frown, because now I'm left unsatisfied, and

I sure as hell am not showing Bardhyl that I need him. He can suffer for all I care.

But before I can get off the bed, Dušan closes the distance, peeling off his shirt. "You're not finished, gorgeous."

His words send a shiver down my spine, and my clit twitches as if it might bring me to orgasm the moment they touch me.

"Agreed." Lucien is next to him, taking off his pants and shirt, his cock erect. I can't stop staring. In seconds, all three are standing over me, naked and palming their cocks. Holy crap… How exactly is this going to work?

"Maybe we should make a bet?" Bardhyl starts, eyeing me. "Let's see if you can resist not coming tonight?"

"Shut up with your stupid bets," I state. "They somehow always lead to you winning."

He winks and smiles coyly. Right now I'm in bed naked, surrounded by sex-starved wolves, and my libido is craving them. And Bardhyl is back to his usual self.

Dušan climbs onto the bed with me, prowling closer, and in a flash, I forget everything. I shudder from the shiver racing over my slick heat.

Guess it's too late to turn back now, isn't it?

This has to be the wildest thing I've ever done, and I'm freaking excited at the prospect of what's about to happen.

I chew on my lower lip, and Dušan is on me in seconds, his mouth on mine. He kisses me with aggression, taking what he wants. I make a strange sound in my throat as I slip under his spell. His body against mine is sizzling. His hand cups my breast, and I moan, pushing my chest toward him. His touch, his kiss, his voice pull at my nerve endings.

Heat flares between my thighs. I'm so horny from what Bardhyl started earlier, and Dušan ignites it back up to another level. His fingers slide down my stomach, over the small mound of hair. I widen my legs, needing him as he shifts to position himself between them.

Lucien and Bardhyl watch like this is a show for them... but they know they're waiting for their turns. And I can't believe I'm so turned on by this. A finger slides into me, then another, and every nerve ending in my body crackles.

I throw my head back, falling onto my back on the bed. My heart pounding, I moan as Dušan fingers me and takes a nipple into his mouth, sucking, gnawing.

Blood rushes south, and I'm so near to bursting from arousal, I don't think I can hold on for much longer. I rock my hips back and forth when Dušan suddenly stops and draws his fingers out.

I protest with a groan as he pulls back and sits on his heels on the bed, eating me with his gaze. His cock is so erect and large, the bulbous tip coated in pre-cum.

"What's going on?" I ask. "Why did you stop?"

He takes my hand and draws me to sit upright. He lies on his back across the bed and tucks his hands behind his head. "You're too close," he tells me.

"And? What's wrong with that?" I purse my lips. He's not resistant to the allure we have, the invisible chemistry that hums between us, the one that makes us fated mates.

"Tonight is for so much more. Tell me what you want me to do," he commands.

"I want you to make me come, to make me scream, to ease the growing ache in my body from how much I need you all."

"Then tell me to fuck you."

I kind of like his dominance more than I ever thought I would.

"Will you fuck me?" I ask, my voice soft and

shaky. I want this, need this. So I don't hesitate to place one leg over his lap and straddle him, his erection grazing across my entrance. He's so smooth and hot, and he reaches up to grab my breasts. It's easy to push myself over his erection. I'm so wet that I slide over him, my walls clenching around him as I lower myself.

As his eyes roll back and a delicious groan builds in his throat, I find my bravery to really do this to my satisfaction. As I inch him into me, I feel myself stretch. I shake while he grasps my waist and bucks his hips up, driving himself further inside.

I cry out with strokes of pain and pleasure. But he can't stop himself, pumping into me, and then I'm riding him, Lucien and Bardhyl staring at my bouncing breasts.

Goosebumps flare over my skin, the friction Dušan generates burning me up from the inside out.

"This is so fucking hot." Lucien growls.

Bardhyl moves to stand at the end of the bed, right alongside us, and he palms his cock.

I angle myself forward, one hand perched on the mattress, the other reaching for Bardhyl's cock. Steel covered in silk, he's so hard and thick. I shift my head toward him, and he steps closer for easier access. He guides his dick into my mouth, tasting salty and strangely sweet. I have half a mind to prank him right now.

But Dušan is pounding into me so hard that I can't think of anything beyond our crazy sex act.

Bardhyl pushes deeper into my mouth and I suck on him. That's when hands clasp my ass, and it takes me a second to realize Lucien is now behind me. I know exactly where this is going.

Dušan slows as Lucien's fingers glide over my ass, using my juices to coat me.

"Babe, you're so wet and ready for me." He glides a finger into my ass and my muscles clench. "So tight. Just let me in, okay?"

I don't answer because I'm sucking on Bardhyl. But when I feel Lucien's tip edging into my puckered ass, I stiffen.

Dušan stokes my breasts, pinching my nipples. An electric buzz runs down my back.

Lucien pushes into me slowly, working his way in without any rush, and I appreciate that so much.

They're so tender with me when needed, and they know just how much pressure to apply when they're savage.

When all three men completely fill me, moisture floods me. They start grinding into me, all of us in a rhythm. I'm throbbing and aching with desire. They hold me up and fuck me while I dig my hands into the blanket, fire flaring on my skin. I've never felt so fulfilled, so right, so wanted.

"You're beautiful," Dušan groans, his hips pounding me, his cock pushing in and out past my pussy's lips.

Lucien's fingers massage my ass cheeks as he takes me from behind. The friction he ignites brings on a different level of exhilaration. Bardhyl's cock fills my mouth, his large hand on my back.

A moan rolls in my throat, and a trembling starts deep within me. Then I explode with an orgasm that slams into me like the most powerful storm. It rips through and takes everything before I even know what's hit me. I convulse, and my body clenches. The men growl and hiss.

Even as I float on my climax, their own happy endings burst forward, flooding me with their seed, the tips of their cocks swelling, knotting and locking in place. Dušan's and Lucien's cocks press against my inner walls, snug and tight in there.

Bardhyl howls, and warmth spills into my mouth as he comes. I swallow him, accept him into me, loving how in this one perfect moment, we are one. And a bit of each of them is now a part of me.

Heat flares over me as the guys' muscles tense. My sex squeezes as I float down from heaven.

Bardhyl pulls out and drops to his knees alongside us, his eyes glazed over as he roars with the explosive arousal. "Oh, cupcake, your mouth is wicked and delicious." His lips are on my shoulder, licking me, nibbling on my flesh, his hand finding a breast.

A sudden, eruptive power comes out of nowhere and sweeps over my body. A dark, all-consuming wolf energy I've never felt before. It crashes through me, punching forward. The combination of my body vibrating and the men filling me, does something to me. My wolf rubs within me, and her sweet smell engulfs me. It's overbearing, to the point where I no longer smell my Alphas.

An ache burrows through me.

The men remain glued beside me. But I'm changing, and a sliver of panic arises in that moment. Will I change while two knotted cocks are wedged inside me?

I whimper with the fear that I can't do this, that

my wolf will overpower me and kill all of us in this perfect moment of ecstasy.

The images of all of us dead haunt me while energy bubbles and slithers down my spine, crawling through me from my head to my toes and everywhere else in between.

Dušan hisses with pleasure beneath me while Lucien's hand grips my ass, but it's only Bardhyl who doesn't make a sound. When I look at him, I see the whiteness of his cheeks. He feels it too…

He starts to stand when Dušan snarls. "Don't fucking break our connection." His voice deepens, and of course, he's sensed the energy between us. How could he not?

Is this the moment I shift? When everything can come to a halting end or a new beginning?

CHAPTER 18

MEIRA

Bardhyl finds my mouth, and he kisses me deeply. Goosebumps spread over my skin as flashes of fiery energy pop over my vision and in my mind.

It escalates quicker. A heat consumes us, and for those few moments, I feel like I'm floating amid the stars with my men, in a place where no one but us exists. But I can't shake the trepidation tensing my muscles that this might be the moment I shift.

My Alphas growl, as if their wolves are responding to my power. Maybe they are. My heart pounds savagely and heat burns me up. Sweat rolls down my spine, and suddenly, the pressure from their knots inside me ease. Yet

Bardhyl's tongue continues to tangle with mine, and our kiss is hypnotic.

I inhale all their scents. I feel them… but what's between us is so much more than physical. There's the faintest stroke of fur against me, as if they are right beside me in their wolf forms. I flip open my eyelids. All three are still human.

Bright light blinks behind my eyes.

In a heartbeat, something snaps inside me.

Crack.

It sounds like bones breaking, but there's no pain, only that constant, annoying light behind my eyes that blinds me. It reminds me in a strange way of the moon…

My wolf rolls around within me, more active than she's ever been. She spreads through me, consuming me.

I open myself to her.

You're safe to come out. Join us.

A swift, sharp pain slashes across my chest, and I shatter. I scream, the pain swelling like someone is pouring acid over my skin.

I cry out, then pass out.

Coldness washes over my brow, and it takes me a few seconds to come to my senses and recall everything.

The Alphas.

Insanely delicious sex.

And something changing in me.

My wolf.

I snap open my eyes and shoot upright, finding myself sitting in bed. Dušan sits next to me, holding a damp towel. Lucien lies at my feet, while Bardhyl is on my other side. They all stare at me with shock in their faces.

I wrench my gaze to a blanket covering me to my waist, but I'm human, and there's no fur in sight.

"What's going on?" I ask, blurry on what happened right at the end of our groups sex.

"You passed out, cupcake."

I look over to Bardhyl, who stays close, still naked, as are the others. He reaches over and pushes away the sweaty hair stuck to the side of my face. His touch is tender and warm, luring me to lean closer and shut my eyes again.

But I shake away the urge, needing to understand.

"Did I change? It felt like maybe I did?"

No one responds at first, and when I meet Dušan's gaze, he shakes his head. "You're a goddess, Meira. The energy your body expelled sent unimaginable strength into our bodies. Your wolf lingered just below the surface. I felt her, called to her. But she never came."

I don't know how to feel. Sorrowful. Disappointed. Scared. Confusion crawls through me as I attempt to piece it all together, chasing away the other emotions.

"The moon," I state and quickly shuffle from the bed, pushing past the guys, the blanket sliding down from around my body. Naked, I hurry to the window and push aside the heavy curtain to stare outside. The first threads of sunlight spear upward from the horizon, staining the sky in oranges and reds. Shadows claim the woodland in the distance.

I scan the heavens for the moon.

"Did you hear something?" Dušan whispers behind me, the heat from his body spreading over me.

"It's only half a moon," I say. "It was so weird. One moment we are all together in bed, then a strange power swept over me, like my wolf would come out. I swore she would, and I sensed the moon calling to me. What went wrong?"

His large hands fall to my hips, drawing me away from the window. He turns me to face him. "A wolf's power comes from the moon, but it doesn't have to be full to affect us. Legend says the first wolf was born during a hunters' moon. A pack of normal wolves savagely attacked a human. She barely clung on to life after the brutal assault. But the only way to save her was with the blessing from the moon. Her energies blended with the energies of the wolves, from their saliva and blood that had seeped into her body. On the next full moon, she changed for the first time into what we are today. She is the first of our kind. Stories say she bore children to nine different men, and they all spread out across the world to populate the land."

I blink at him. "Is that a true story?"

He shrugs. "It's an origin myth, but while the details are sketchy, we do grow stronger on full moons and become more animalistic. Any wounds we have heal instantly on those nights. But our transformations aren't influenced by the moon's phases."

"Then why didn't my change work?" I breathe

the words, barely a whisper. My throat thickens, feeling like I'm always fighting to barely keep my head above the waves. Nothing I do gives me a fucking break.

Dušan slides a hand to the side of my face, drawing me closer. "We are so close, gorgeous. Tomorrow we will all bond again, building the energy between us. And we'll do it again and again until she comes out. Together we'll guide your wolf to emerge safely."

Doubt dances around in my mind as I recall the sharp pain that sliced through me when I thought she was coming out. Something held her back. "What if—"

"No," Dušan insists. "I could practically touch her. In the next week, you are transforming."

His confidence is heartwarming, and I desperately want to believe he's right. I sweep my focus to Lucien and Bardhyl, who stand by the bed, looking at us, expecting something I can't give. I feel like I've let them down, yet Dušan has so much hope in his eyes that I remain quiet.

His slow, circular movements on my back ease the worry for now. "Come. We'll all get dressed and leave. We'll arrive home soon, and everything will be good once more."

Either he's convinced himself that I'm already saved, or he's doing an amazing job of sounding like he carries no doubts.

My heart thunders in my ears while coldness drops through me. But I don't voice my fears. Instead, I respond with a forced smile.

On the inside, my thoughts chant, *Please let my wolf come. Let her not kill me in the process.*

Dušan

The midday sun blares down on us. We've been walking since dawn. We come across no rogue wolves or packs, and the few undead we encountered were too far away to catch up to us.

"When we get back, I vote for us all having a group bath in our pool," Lucien suggests, his gaze all for Meira.

She's beautiful, captivating, and scared as hell. She smiles cheerfully, but it's all pretend. I see it in the tightness around her mouth, I smell it in the perspiration that's heavier than it'd normally be at our walking pace. Her chest rises and falls like the rush of the rampant river.

"Agreed. So it shall be," Bardhyl replies. "Meira, I will teach you to duck swim. Even if you don't know how to swim, this will help."

Meira cuts him a confused look and her light laugh is genuine. She truly adores the men, and they bring out a playful side in her, which I love.

"I'm not picturing this duck swim," she answers. "Don't they just float on top of the water and kick their legs underneath?"

"Lucien taught it to me once."

Lucien chuckles, slapping a hand to Bardhyl's back. "It's not a fucking duck. I told you that before, man. It's called butterfly breast-stroking, and it's one of the most difficult styles to learn and master."

Bardhyl scoffs, but he claims he can do anything before he's tried it.

"Do butterflies even swim?" Meira asks, her brow arching.

"It's just the technique, the arm movements in the water depict their wings," I explain. "But I do agree, swimming might help strengthen and build endurance for when your wolf comes out."

She drags her gaze from Lucien and Bardhyl to

me. "I agree to a pool party, and I'm sure I will pick up this swimming technique easily." Her eyes challenge Bardhyl.

The three of them break into chatter, but I'm struggling to focus on anything but last night's events.

Her hope was shattered when she discovered she hadn't transformed. It'd been heartbreaking to watch her expression crumble. I won't deny I had my hopes up that she would experience her first shift last night. The energy lifted all the hairs on my body; my wolf bounced inside me frantically for her release.

But she never did… Why the fuck not?

I say nothing about my worries. Not until I have time to look into her blood results and understand what piece of the puzzle I'm missing.

We aren't far from the compound, and these woods are familiar now. I couldn't be happier to be surrounded by my pack and the safety of our walls. I'll deal with Mad and his bullshit after I heal Meira. That's my priority.

I listen to them ramble about swimming, and I realize that maybe sharing her with my two closest pack members and friends will work out better than I expected. Though there will be some nights

I'll want her completely for myself and no damn sharing will be happening.

The trees thin the closer we get to the compound, and already I can see the top of the old fortress in the distance. I can't keep the smile off my face. I never thought I'd be so happy to be home.

A sudden, heavy scent of wet dog fur and freshly turned soil, finds me on the breeze that whistles past us. My hackles bristle. Wolves.

Bardhyl and Lucien ease back, Meira between them.

Dead silence floods the woods.

I cut my men a look of concern. "Keep her close."

I smell it again, and I sniff the air, confirming it's Ash Wolves. Before I can respond, movement from my right draws my attention.

"Dušan," a male commands, the voice familiar. When the stranger emerges from the shadows of the forest, it's Danu, a Beta I recognize. I've spoken to him maybe once or twice before. My pack grows weekly, and I try to do the rounds to familiarize myself with everyone, but he's a recent recruit. He stands twenty feet away, tall and lanky with short, golden hair. He stares at us like a stunned deer.

"Did something happen to you?" I ask, closing the distance between us.

He doesn't respond but looks scared, his shoulders drooping forward, panic flashing in his gaze.

A low snarl reverberates in my head that something is wrong.

An unexpected explosion of thunderous footsteps drum behind me like a storm.

I pivot around to discover a dozen Ash Wolves in human form charging at us from all around. Members I've enjoyed a meal with, shared a beer with... Now anger warps their expressions toward us. I'm fucking confused about what is going on, and I react too slowly.

Bardhyl whips around, but one Beta has jumped onto his back, the other kicking his legs out from under him. He snarls, his arms flying as he loses his balance and hits the ground on his knees. The Beta on his back injects a syringe into his neck. The Viking pushes them aside with a wild swing of his arm, sending them off their feet. He clutches the side of his neck and stumbles before falling to his knees and flat on his face.

Fuck!

I lunge toward them, roaring, my pulse on overdrive, while Lucien drags Meira to safety. She's stumbling to get away, her eyes wide at the unwarranted attack.

But it's too late. Others crash-tackle Lucien and shove her to the ground. He attacks one of them, but three more jump on him. Meira frantically scrambles to her feet and picks up a branch as a weapon.

I charge and whip my arm around Meira's waist, wrenching her to my side.

"What the hell is going on?" she murmurs.

I back away from the dozen Ash Wolves, members who are supposed to be loyal to me. Lucien lies on the ground, buried under three men, Bardhyl passed out from whatever drugs they injected him with.

Ice fills my veins.

"You will pay with your life for this deceit." I growl, fully aware that we've been ambushed. How long have they waited out here for our return?

Meira is tucked against my side. I'll rip apart every one of these fuckers if they touch her.

I scan their faces, memorizing each one for when I come for them. Rein meets my gaze... a younger man whom I saved from the undead and brought into our compound. He'd lost his family to the creatures. His attention flicks from me to the woods at my side.

I jerk around and my throat closes.

Mad.

My fucking stepbrother emerges from the shadowy woodlands. His ice blue eyes pierce into me, white-blond hair fluttering in the breeze. He's dressed immaculately in pressed pants, boots, and… is that my white button-up shirt? Rage echoes through me.

"What the fuck have you done?" I nudge Meira behind me and lift my chin, my hands curling into fists. I want to rip the smirk off his face.

I should have killed him the moment he returned to the compound. Should have known he'd have allies. Should have been smarter, but finding my fated mate was my priority. It was also a deadly distraction.

"Brother, you took your time returning. Glad you brought the bitch back."

I spit on the ground between us. "I'll tear your spine out if you touch her."

Except it's too late. I see our fate in his hateful smirk, in us being trapped by wolves who've betrayed me. My stomach twists in on itself at the thought of what Mad must have offered them to convert to his side. The promise of immunity against the undead?

Meira is suddenly wrenched from my grasp, her cries ringing in the air.

I spin and lunge after the two men seizing her from me. She screams, one of her arms flinging free from her captors and reaching for me. The dread on her face will stay with me for eternity.

My wolf claws for release to destroy them. All I see is red and their deaths as I run to her, barely inches from claiming her back.

"Dušan!" Meira calls to me, her gaze on something behind me.

In that moment, a hard punch connects with the middle of my back, sending me sprawling forward on hands and knees. I try to get up, but Mad locks an iron arm around my neck, keeping me down.

"She's no longer yours," he whispers in my ear, his voice gravelly and flooded with wry mirth.

Murder plays on my mind. How much I will enjoy taking his life. I tremble with fury and thrust against him. But everything dissolves when I watch Rein jab a needle into the side of Meira's neck.

Her cries cut me.

I explode, my wolf pushing to tear out of me.

The sharp prick of a needle jammed into my neck comes fast, as do the tingles that rush through my limbs. Then the numbness hits.

Mad drives a fist into my shoulder, just as I'd done to him back at the pack house fortress. I collapse forward. My heart beats hysterically as I crash to the ground, devastation fueling my rage.

The world sits sideways in my view as I lie on the ground. Meira is on hands and knees, gasping for air like she's choking.

My mouth opens, but only a gurgled sound comes out.

She's screaming with agony, her back arching. Skin splitting and fur spilling out, her bones stretching, her jaw elongating.

The change has come now.

Oh, shit!

Straining, I shove myself up to my feet. The world spins and I can't even feel my body. Adrenaline owns me, and I grasp onto those moments. I need to get to her. Connect with her energy to help her shift.

Meira!

Her gaze finds me, and behind those wolf eyes

lies my little gorgeous girl. Her panic calls to me, fueling the fear that curls around my heart that she won't survive the change, that the wolf will kill her.

Growling under my breath, I push my numb legs to move forward so I can see her through her first transformation. One step and someone strikes me in the back of my head. My vision dances with stars.

I roar and slam to the ground like a sack. I'm fucking useless, and it's killing me to hear her screams.

Shadows feather the edges of my vision. Darkness comes for me, but I fight whatever Mad injected into me. I tense up and push harder against the toxin in my veins.

I hold on to Meira's gaze, though my muscles refuse to respond, to help me get up again.

She thrusts and fights the change. Mad and his minions are standing around, watching her. She's mid-transformation, her cries like blades to my throat. First changes are gruesome and fucking excruciating. All I want is to take her into my arms as she shifts. To help her through this.

The fire inside me grows uncontrollably.

Everything we've done to help her has been for nothing.

Her shredded clothes lay by her feet and she shakes herself, dragging herself up in her wolf form… a tawny, reddish pelt, round ears darker in color. She's not a huge wolf, but she's spectacular. Her eyes are pale with only a tinge of bronze, except I no longer see any sign of my Meira behind them.

My heart cracks in half, the agony slicing my insides, and all I can think about is her smile, her laughter, her body against mine. The joy she brought me will ruin me. I can't go on without her by my side.

Please don't let the wolf have killed my sweet Meira.

Seconds is all it takes for her to scan her surroundings and sniff the air.

A fraction of time for her to snarl at the two men lunging for her.

Lips peeled back, she growls with immense fierceness and turns on them with a aggression only comparable to Bardhyl's. She is nothing like Meira.

The wolf tears right into Rein and rips out half his stomach with one vicious bite.

A split second later, and she's on the rampage for the others.

Screams and a wild battle begins.

If the wolf has completely taken her over and she's gone, she will kill us all. If I manage to somehow survive this, I swear on my life that I will destroy every last fucking asshole who stood against us on this day.

For you Meira, I will burn down this world.

Thank you for reading Shadowlands Sector Two

Reviews are super important to authors as it helps other reader make better decisions on books they will read. So if you have a moment, please do leave a review on Amazon.

Start Reading Shadowlands Sector Three today!

Discover more books from Mila Young and find your Happily Ever After at www.milayoungbooks.com

ABOUT MILA YOUNG

Best-selling author, Mila Young tackles everything with the zeal and bravado of the fairytale heroes she grew up reading about. She slays monsters, real and imaginary, like there's no tomorrow. By day she rocks a keyboard as a marketing extraordinaire. At night she battles with her mighty pen-sword, creating fairytale retellings, and sexy ever after tales. In her spare time, she loves pretending she's a mighty warrior, walks on the beach with her dogs, cuddling up with her cats, and devouring every fantasy tale she can.

For more information...
milayoungarc@gmail.com

Join my Wicked Readers Group

facebook.com/groups/milayoungwickedreaders

www.ingramcontent.com/pod-product-compliance
Lightning Source LLC
Chambersburg PA
CBHW051253210726

48287CB00002B/476